"THE BELT OF KINGS"

ANTHONY BUNKO

Anthony Bunko

Copyright © 2004 Anthony Bunko

The right of Anthony Bunko to be identified as the Author of the work has been asserted by him in accordance with the Copyright, Designs and Patent Act, 1988

All the creepy-crawlies in this book are fictitious (even Eric and his orange fingernails), and any resemblance to actual insects, living, dead or kinetically frozen, is purely coincidental.

All rights reserved. No part of this publication may be reproduced, stored in a retrieval system, or transmitted, in any form or by any means without the prior written permission of the publisher, nor be otherwise circulated in any form of binding or cover other than that in which it is published and without similar conditions being imposed on the subsequent purchaser.

ISBN 0-9547273-1-2

First published 2005 by A. Bunko, 17 Cyfarthfa Gardens, Merthyr. CF48 2SE

Printed and Bound by:- Creative Print and Design, Wales

www.anthonybunko.co.uk
Email:- anthony@bunko.freeserve.co.uk

Dedicated to:-

"My daughters (Danielle & Georgia) and their unquenchable thirst for making friends, buying new clothes, and MTV"

Anthony Bunko

Other titles by Anthony Bunko

The Tale of the Sh-gging Monkeys

The Tale of Two Sh-gging Monkeys
The Siege of El Rancho

The Belt of Kings

Contents   *Page no.*

01. Lambs in wolves clothing	07
02. Cree-season	19
03. The invasion of the Emperor	27
04. Under pier 14	35
05. Nut-cracker suite	43
06. Entering 'Buzztown'	49
07. On the frozen playground	69
08. The Emperor decides on supper	81
09. Snatch and Grub	89
10. Something's wrong	95
11. Finding Uncle Paddy	101
12. Cocooned	117
13. The rat trap	123
14. Falling apart at the seams	133
15. The plot gets thicker	137
16. Costume changes	147
17. The banana skins	157
18. Things turn flaky	163
19. Terry the woodlouse is big leggy	173
20. The magnificent three	183
21. Now it's the magnificent six	199
22. Sunnytime blues	213
23. Here comes the……	219

Anthony Bunko

Chapter 1

'Lambs in wolves clothing'

The large cargo ship, which was bursting to the seams with bananas, appeared through the mist and sailed into the safe waters of the harbour that surrounded Tiger-Moth Bay.

To announce its arrival it sent out a loud blast from its hooter that caused poor Bongo to nearly jump out of his skin. The noise from the old rusty vessel reverberated around the bustling crowded quayside like a belch from a drunken sailor who had spent all of his shore leave immersed in a barrel of cloudy ale.

The bitterly cold wind blew through every nook and cranny, and Bongo found himself frozen to the spot, unable to move.

His little heart beat wildly as he hid behind some discarded boxes which had once housed juicy, ripe oranges, transported to the docks from some far away land.

As Bongo hid in the shadows he observed his older brother busily searching for supplies amongst the pile of rubbish which blew back and forth on the bad breath of the north wind.

Although he was in disguise, Bongo knew that it was still a very dangerous and hostile place to hang out. He had heard many grisly tales and had been told stories about how even the giant people, who normally stomped about day and night, in deadly, leather shoes, would tread ever so carefully through these cold streets around the dockside, usually glancing nervously over their shoulders in case of attack.

'Hey, Bongo! Stop acting like a frightened girly worm and get over here and give us a hand with this,' his brother whispered, while struggling to drag some rich, juicy morsel from out of a chink in the pavement.

Bongo looked left, then right, and even straight up, before zigzagging from the relative safety of his hiding place to go and help his brother with the new found treasure.

The rain slashed across his path as he unintentionally danced through a freshly formed puddle. He didn't normally mind the harsh weather, but the heavens hadn't stopped crying for what seemed like several lifetimes.

He accepted that his memory wasn't the biggest or sharpest. Bongo knew that the big, shiny, yellow thing that dried up the rain and sat smiling up in the big blue thing hadn't shown its face around these parts since long before his mother had given birth to his fifty-six brothers and thirty-two sisters.

He hadn't felt the warmth on his four pairs of eyes since long before the sad day that his father had gone to fight the Eastside cockroaches and had not returned. He remembered with regret how his entire family had slowly shuffled off to the little church on that afternoon, locked their many legs together and prayed for their brave dad's safe return.

But as the season changed, and the long dark nights closed in like a curtain engulfing the city known as Dublin, it was left to Bongo and his brother to take over the mantle as the father figures, providing protection and food for the rest of the family.

This grown-up responsibility sat comfortably on the broad, and more street-wise shoulders, of his brother. But unfortunately Bongo wasn't anywhere near as strong, or, sometimes, as foolish as his older sibling. In fact, being a healthy teenager, he just wanted to go and enjoy himself all day with his mates, instead of scampering and tip-toeing around in scary places, hiding in the shadows from frightening creatures who wouldn't think twice of making him the main course of a tasty snack.

But times were desperate and food was hard to come by. The land was covered by an invisible disease called 'A Depression', which, although it couldn't be seen by the naked eye, was often evident on the wrinkles and worry-lines of the faces of giants and insects alike.

Even his family's favourite weekend dish of roasted flies on bread crumbs had ceased. The flies themselves were not worth the effort of catching. They were too thin with the hunger, and had little, if any, meat on their bones.

So, because of this, there was little spare time for Bongo to feel sorry for himself and to indulge in the normal activities that teenager spiders got up to. Regretfully, there were more important things to do, and there were many, many mouths to feed… and feed… and feed ….and feed.

Back on the dockside, the two brothers wrestled awkwardly with the object, afraid of making any unnecessary noises or sudden movements that would draw attention to themselves.

This was Beetle territory and the Black Pats (as they were unaffectionately known in the other section of the Bay) were not partial to a couple of scallywag spiders sneaking around their patch, in disguise, with the devious intention of pilfering the already scarce crumbs of food from their patch.

'Keep your beetle mask on,' his brother instructed Bongo, and clipped him behind his ear.

'But it's too hot! I can't breathe in this costume,' Bongo replied.

'Do as I say! This place will be swarming with the nasty hard shelled pests any time now,' his brother angrily hissed at him before spying a large drinking tavern a couple of doors down, which was usually frequented every single minute of every long day and longer night, by the giant people.

'Hey Bro…. Where did you get these costumes from, anyway?' Bongo asked, as he immediately followed his brother's instructions and replaced the mask.

'Old Mister Zimmermann, the silk-worm, made them for me.'

'They are excellent quality. The best I've ever seen. How much did you have to pay for them?' Bongo asked, while trying to align his own eyes with the eye sockets in the suit. It wasn't easy.

'Nothing,' his brother snapped back.

'Nothing?' If Bongo's brother could have seen his face underneath the mask, he would have seen signs of it being slightly confused at his brother's earlier comment.

'Yeah! You heard me correctly. I just told him that if he made them for me… I wouldn't eat his little nephews,' he declared coldly, before adding, 'Bongo, now wait here, and don't get into any trouble. I'm going to get us some of that strange liquid that the giant people drink. The stuff that makes them sing out of tune and walk funny.'

Before Bongo had a chance to challenge him even more about the way he obtained the suits, his brother (who was also disguised as a beetle) scampered towards the large swinging doors of the tavern, which had been designed (unsuccessfully) to keep out the cold wind (which howled around the dockside) and to ensure that the music stopped inside.

Bongo wished that he had the same ruthless streak as his older brother.

He often wondered what it would be like if he was suave, sophisticated, and respected by his peers. Sadly he was just a spotty, teenage arachnid, with a bad chest, and eight knobbly knees that had only just started to sprout bum fluff.

He gasped in horror as he witnessed his brother narrowly miss getting squashed by a couple of giant people who had tumbled out of the tavern and were rolling on the floor in some sort of bear hug.

The younger spider waited nervously in the shadows, eyes rotating in all directions at once.

He knew that most of the beetles would have seen the arrival of the new ship carrying bananas. They would have sailed out on small pieces of wood to meet it in order to see what goodies were on board, before the alley cats and the woodlice clambered all over it and fleeced the lot.

Bongo held on tightly to the almost rotten potato peeling that would thankfully feed his starving family for at least a week.

His breath got shorter. His chest became tighter. He needed to take the stupid beetle mask off before he had one of his attacks. He loosened the straps and double checked that his brother was out of sight.

'That's better,' he silently mouthed to the vegetable, while sucking in the damp salty atmosphere, the sort that hangs around every shipping port throughout the world.

He suddenly froze. He heard a skittering sound from the drainpipe by his left hand side.

He realised that he didn't have time to put his mask back on. He imagined the worst. And the worst thing to imagine at that moment in time was a battalion of Beatnik beetles (the hardest and most vicious of the species) appearing one by one, through the guttering. He imagined them finding him all alone, half-dressed as one of them, holding a sliver of potato peeling, and in the throws of having an asthma attack.

'Why didn't I listen to my brother?' Bongo cursed to himself. 'Now I'm going to get beaten to a pulp and probably have my legs plucked.'

He quickly made the sign of the cross with all eight legs, pulled his cap over his eyes and waited to be ripped apart.

As he offered up his prayers he remembered being told in spider school about the terrible atrocities carried out by the beetles during the Great Five Week War of Salmon Street, just across from the Old Bakery.

Bongo started to physically shake on the spot as he recalled being shown a sketch in an old book. It was of a pack of black soldier beetles, systemically pulling the legs off a defenceless spider. He'd had nightmares for six months after that and wet his bed at least three times a week. The picture had reminded him of some poor dandelion flower losing its precious white seeds in the windiest storm that the spring could muster.

'Hello Bongo.' The young spider heard a familiar voice and felt a cold, wet snout touching his hairy face. 'Going to a fancy dress party, are you? Who's that dressed in the potato peeling costume?' the owner of the voice joked, before letting out a deep cackle that raced up the drainpipe and escaped into the night sky.

Bongo was disorientated and very confused. He slowly opened his eyes to see if what was in front of him made sense.

'Hi Duggan…. I'm so glad to bump into you,' the spider muttered thankfully, on seeing his mate.

Duggan the rat, (who incidentally didn't have a tail) was standing there as large as life and smiling at him.

Now, it must be explained before this story continues and the plot thickens (like gravy in a saucepan), why Duggan the rat didn't have a tail to call his own.

Now, anyone who just happened to noticed a rat with no tail scurrying through the poorly lit streets, must have thought it was slightly strange and a bit of a mystery.

But it wasn't at all strange in the slightest, or even a mystery as far as Bongo, and most of the other insects that populated these parts were concerned. They had all heard Duggan's full and often colourful, explanations a thousand times and usually, each time the rodent told it, a different ending would escape from his lips. Everyone knew that the rat was renowned for telling lies, and in fact, had been labelled with the amusing nickname of 'The King-rat of exaggerating the truth'.

The tailless rat's new, favourite, and probably his most unconvincing fable, of how he had lost his tail, was that it had been bitten off in a mammoth scrap with a pack of tom-cats in an alleyway behind the iron mongers shop. But everyone who came into contact with the friendly and extremely talkative rat knew that Duggan couldn't punch his way out of a wet paper bag.

The truth of the matter, and the real reason for the rat's lack of the six inches of skin that should have followed him wherever he went, was that he had been born that way, along with his twin brother Ernie, who had sadly died at birth, and his aunty Lucy, who had been caught by the rat-catchers during the Black plague of 1923 (but obviously she hadn't been snagged in the traps by her tail).

'Are you on duty tonight?' Bongo asked the happy-go-lucky rat.

'Yes… just started,' Duggan replied, pointing to his hat, where the 'for hire' sign was illuminating up his cheerful face.

'Oh,' said Bongo, looking despondent.

The spider knew that neither of the brothers had any money to pay for a ride. He glanced over to the tavern to see if there was any sign of his big brother.

The two giant people were still wrestling about in the muddy street.

'Ask me where I've been then….. go on… Ask me where I've been then!' Duggan said merrily. He flicked the spider with his cold nose for the second time in as many minutes.

At that moment in time Bongo was more concerned with his safety, but he shrugged his many shoulders blades, and through clenched teeth he muttered, 'Ok… where have you been, Duggan?'

Bongo hadn't quite finished the last bit of the sentence before the rodent, who couldn't hold back his excitement any longer, burst head-first into telling his spider friend the entire story, which had obviously been bubbling up inside him all night.

Duggan was quick to relay to his mate how he had earlier been on a date with the most beautiful rat princess that God had ever put breath into. Apparently, she had just arrived on these shores on a ship whose final destination was a place called America.

'She's from Africa, you know. Her father was the chief rat of a colony that lived underneath a village in Zambolo. You should have seen the size of the zebra bone in his snout. And it was real!'

Bongo was dying to ask the love-struck vermin what the hell a beautiful African rat princess, whose father was the chief rat of a colony, who lived underneath a village in Zambolo, and had a real zebra bone in his snout, would be doing going out with a tailless rodent, who worked part-time for his uncle's taxis service, (Ride-a-Rodent cabs), but, Bongo decided to hold on tightly to that question until another time.

Instead, he just nodded politely. He knew from bitter experience that Duggan was prone to exaggerating the truth more than any other creature in the land. Bongo also realised that the rat got very upset and sulked if anyone challenged his stories. Bongo didn't argue, he just decided to listen.

'Hey... what did I tell you about taking that damn beetle mask off?' Bongo's brother yelled, while dragging a small tobacco leaf behind him, which was full to the brim with a dark liquid.

He put the leaf down and continued his verbal attack on Bongo. 'I swear.... I'll weld that mask to your head next time,'

'Sorry,' Bongo apologised, 'but.... but....'

'Shut up... I don't want any excuses. Do you appreciate how dangerous it is around here?' His words were short and sharp. 'And I promised our Mam that I would look after you.'

'I said I was sorry.' Bongo put the mask on again and instantly turned back into a beetle.

His brother then spotted the rat. 'Hello Duggan; are you on duty tonight?' he asked hopefully.

'Yes,' Duggan replied, a big wide grin covered his smug, whiskery face.

Bongo had a sneaky feeling as to what was coming next, but before he had chance to warn his brother, Duggan sang out his words, 'So ask me where I've been then, go on, ask me where I've been.'

Bongo's brother was one of the sharpest spiders to ever walk around on eight pads. He was street wise with a capital S. He didn't suffer fools and he could usually sniff an opportunity out from over a hundred paces away.

'I'll tell you what Duggan?' he winked at Bongo, 'we can't pay you but if you give us a lift home, you can tell us all about it.'

The excited rat immediately offered his snout as a walkway, which led to the little red seat that was positioned on his back.

He switched off the 'on duty' sign, and the two tired spiders placed their swag to one side, stripped off their costumes, and dozed off. Duggan went on to explain in great detail about his wonderful night with the African rat princess, whose father was the chief of a rat colony that lived underneath a village in Zambolo, and who had a real zebra bone through his nose.

Chapter 2

'Cree- Season'

Bongo woke up in the attic room of an old, worn-out, giant's boot that looked and smelt as though its previous owner must have walked around Dublin a million times before being thrown away.

It was not as grand as the 'Old fishing boat tipped upside down' palace that the insect mayor resided in, but it was still water-proof, and it had been his family's home for several years now.

The teenage spider turned over and snuggled back under the sheets. He tried hard to get back to sleep. He had been having a wonderful dream about flying. That was not unusual. He always dreamt of flying, nearly every night, and fantasised about it most days.

In this dream he imagined that he was gliding high above the Smokey city, with wings as wide as the river and as brightly coloured as a rainbow.

It had always been one of his life-long secret ambitions, along with learning to swim.

Of course, being a true-blooded Irish spider, it was something that he couldn't tell anyone else about. 'A spider wanting to fly' was something of a taboo subject, which was frowned upon amongst the eight legged creatures and was never ever discussed in great detail.

There were other types of insects that apparently had similar fantasies. He had heard how bluebottles would daydream about spinning a web to catch a spider. Bongo laughed at that. He had also been told the sad tale about a moth who liked sitting alone in the dark. These weird stories of the insect underworld were kept quiet and no one really mentioned them.

Bongo just knew that one day his dream would come true and he would fly high above the buildings of Dublin city and look down on the world.

In his bed that morning he stretched out his legs. He rubbed the sleep out of the corners of his many eyes, and then sprang out of the home-made web hammock which was fastened through the boot holes that had once been used to house the laces.

Bongo could sense that something was different. The hairs on his legs were tingling. The air smelt less damp. It had more of a dry, sweet smell to it.

He could hear his many little brother and sister spiderlings way down below, talking (all at once, as usual) while running around mischievously.

The Belt of Kings

Bongo pulled back the tongue of the leather shoe and jumped back in total surprise. He found himself completely flabbergasted. There, smiling back at him from way up in the big blue thing, where the birds flew (which, of course, was different to the big, blue, wet thing that the ships sailed on), was the big, shiny, yellow thing which sometimes lit up the city. It was like a big ball of fire that had a wide grin beaming across its big round face.

'Its sunnytime.... Its sunnytime,' Bongo heard someone yelling loudly.

He looked down and saw a centipede dancing merrily through the narrow streets, arm-in-arm with a large ginger-haired earwig.

His eyes searched around for more evidence, and then he also allowed himself to bellow out the joyous news from the boot-tops.

'Was it true?' Bongo thought. 'Was it really sunnytime already?'

The signs looked good, which ever way his eyes turned.

He couldn't see any puddles of rain on the pavements that would usually reflected his good-looking face back up towards the big blue thing. There wasn't a sight of a dock-leaf umbrella being carried by female insects, rushing around with their weekly shopping. There was not even a hint of greyness in the big blue thing. The place was full to the brim with colour and smiling faces as far as his many sets of eyes could see.

Bongo really, really hoped that it was sunnytime, just as the happy centipede had announced. He knew that if it was actually the first day of the warm spell, then that meant it was officially Cree-season; and Cree-season meant absolute paradise for a teenage insect in Tiger-Moth Bay.

'Mam... Mam... its Cree-season.... Its Cree-season,' Bongo yelled out, putting his cap on his head, while searching under his hammock for his instrument.

His mother was downstairs, shooing the infants out of the front door.

She wiped her hands on her apron and replied, 'I know... I know. Thank God for that. At least now all you kids can go and play outside while the big, shiny, yellow thing is smiling and leave me alone to do some housework. This boot needs a good sunnytime cleaning from tip to toe... starting in your room, my boy.'

Now, for all the creatures, including you giant people in the big wide world that haven't quite worked out what Cree-season is yet, it is probably a good time for another explanation before we move on. Well you see Cree-season is a short time that occurs once a year, and lasts from the time the rain stops falling from the big blue thing, until the cold, white, round flakes of snow replaces it several weeks later.

It is a fantastic time for all the creepy-crawlies that usually fight fang and nail, against each other during the dark months around Tiger-Moth Bay.

Unlike any other place, (including the land where the giant people live), Cree-season has been made law amongst the insects in Dublin.

It had been sanctioned many moons ago by all the most powerful heads of the insect families, so that they would all work and live together during the warm days, stocking up with food and supplies for the long winter months. Fighting, squabbling, and anything else nasty, which would normally be carried out by the dockside creatures, were officially banned.

Cree-season had first started way back during the harsh winter of 1917, when the food supplies became so scarce that nearly half the insect population of the Dublin perished through starvation. Apparently, the winter was so severe, that baby insects died in their mother's arms. Old-aged creatures wrapped in blankets were found frozen to death in their nests or hideaways.

The heads of the seven main insect families…spiders, beetles, centipedes, woodlice, ants, earwigs and bluebottles, were all summoned to an emergency meeting. After hours upon hours of deliberation, the Cree-season treaty of Tiger-Moth Bay was finally drawn up and signed by all the family heads (except for the woodlice, who couldn't write, and instead their representative made her mark by rolling in the ink across the paper).

The rules in the treaty stated:-

1. There would be no fighting between the different species during the time when the big, shiny, round yellow thing sat overhead in the big blue thing.
2. Whoever was the elected mayor at that time (whatever the breed), would have full power and control over the city and would oversee the safe-keeping of all the different types of insect residence, and also ensure that the magical 'Belt of Kings' was guarded at all times. *(This year Terry the bilingual woodlouse had the honour of representing the insect population. He was solely and personally responsible for insisting that point number three was wisely added to the list immediately).*
3. During Cree-season, there would be no drawing pictures on the wall or calling each other nasty insect names, especially 'earthbelly' or 'low-down bum', which had special reference to the woodlice population, who were so often the butt of all the jokes of the other insects.
4. Cree-season would officially stop as soon as the first droplets of cold, white stuff fell from the big blue thing. At that point in time, all the insects would go back to looking out for themselves.

After a brief and successful trial period, even the seagulls and other smaller birds signed up to the treaty. But this was only after Cyril the seagull, their union representative, had negotiated that the bird fraternity were fully allowed to hunt for the slimy, smelly, fishy things that swam in the big, wet, blue thing that the ships sailed on, during the time when the big, shiny, yellow thing smiled over the bay.

It was also written that everything changed during the wintertime. Then the seagulls and birds would only be allowed to scavenge on the land, leaving the slimy, smelly, fishy things several months to recuperate, and do a spot of white water surfing in safety.

Back in the giant's boot called 'home', Bongo rushed out of the front door, clutching a small set of drums under his arms. He pushed past his mother, who was down on her knees scrubbing the doorstep, and he headed into the glorious sunshine.

'Where are you going Bongo?' his mother shouted after him, 'you haven't finished cleaning your room yet.'

'Sorry Mam, but I've got to go. It's Cree-season, and I need to capture someone really special to spend the sunnytime with me.'

Bongo disappeared around the old Chinese linen basket and into the bustling crowded gutter-ways that led to the centre of Tiger-Moth bay.

Anthony Bunko

Chapter 3

'The invasion of the Emperor'

Out on the strangely calm sea of the harbour, in the dark bowels of the recently arrived banana ship, ten banana spiders marched with perfect timing and rhythm, while dragging a bruised and bloody beetle behind them.

The uniformed procession of insects' halted in front of a large wooden crate and the poor, bound and blindfolded beetle was thrown roughly to the floor.

The leader of the scout-party of spiders knocked on the wooden crate.

After a short while, a door on the front of the crate was opened by an extremely large and muscular Goliath tarantula spider, called Bollo, who, without really trying, filled the entrance.

Bollo was the type of creature that didn't need to speak. One look from the colossal spider-beast was enough to ask any question he liked, without actually talking.

'Please, Bollo, could you inform the master we've caught another one?' the spider who had knocked on the door asked.

Bollo could immediately tell by the shaky tone of the insect's voice that he was intimidated by the large spider, whose role it was to not only guard the entrance, but to also protect the Emperor with his life (or more likely the life of other smaller creatures) that threatened to cross his path.

'Hope he's knows more than that other one?' Bollo the large spider grunted.

They both looked across to where a crab was tied up to a pillar. The shellfish appeared to have two black eyes and a bloodied nose.

'He stinks the place out. He smells of rotten fish and body odour.' Bollo the spider shook his head, before scuttling slowly off into the darkest corner of the box.

A few minutes later, the entire front of the crate was lowered. It landed with a thud onto the ship's decking.

The blindfold was removed from the beetle. It took him a few seconds for his eyes to readjust to the light. Then, all of a sudden, he saw a big, black ball inside the crate. He had wrongly assumed it would be filled with green, unripe bananas.

It took the beetle a while to notice that the big, black ball was actually moving and rolling towards him. He gasped in horror as he realised that the black ball was made up of thousands of the deadly

South American banana spiders (the most feared, blackest, and hairiest spiders on the planet).

The beetle felt his hard skin develop goose-pimples as he observed the moving ball of insects split apart. They automatically formed a menacing circle around him and his captives. Bollo, the big muscular spider, banged on the side of the crate with a matchstick. All heads turned towards the noise. The sound of silence quickly prevailed over the room.

As the circle of giant spiders closed in, the beetle saw a very dark spider sitting erect on a large throne in the centre of the crate. The beetle assumed that the dark spider had to be royalty. He was as black as the darkest night with a set of red, evil eyes, that pierced the gloom, like rubies sparkling deep inside a cave.

Every set of eyes in the place watched as their master, known as Emperor Balasz purposefully rose up from the throne and stood to attention. The beetle noticed that this royal spider didn't appear that big in physical size, but he seemed to possess a huge presence. He was different to the rest of them. He wasn't quite as big, and was less hairy, but somehow looked a lot more fearsome.

Now the main reason that Emperor Balasz was different was, although he had grown up in the rain forest of darkest South America, his family were originally from Eastern Europe. His great grandfather (who was a Hungarian Romany gipsy-spider) had left a life of poverty on the streets of Budapest, in search of wealth in warmer climes.

Luckily for Balasz, his mother (an attractive dark-haired beauty) had been hand-picked to mate with the late Emperor of the rain forest, the great tarantula called Edi. After the rumpy-pumpy event, and in the well-trusted tradition of the black widow spider, she proceeded to murder, and then eat her lover, accompanied by an egg-plant salad, and washed down with a large glass of red grape juice.

She was immediately pronounced Queen Spider of the entire country. Not long after, Balasz was born and became heir to the throne.

Even as a young spiderling Balasz was different, not only in appearance, but also in his evil ambition. This ambition was only matched by his fascination for power and everything shiny. He was destined for greatness. He was not only black in colour but also in deed and mind. By the time of his third moult, he had already murdered the other male spiders in the pack, and had plotted his two-year plan to conquer the world. By his fifth birthday he was the most feared insect in the land, with a killer army that carried out his every command.

Back in the depths of the banana boat, he was flanked on each side by two enormous spiders. They made Bollo the bodyguard appear small. They had muscles where muscles shouldn't have been. In their front legs they gripped firmly onto dangerous-looking pine-cones, with tips as sharp as any dressmaker's pins.

What the confused and petrified beetle couldn't see by observation alone (unless he could have peeked up their loin cloths) was that the two huge spiders had willingly sacrificed their man-hood (or insect-hood), in the sacred name of the Emperor. Their main role in life was purely to protect the emperor's harem of lady spiders during the trip.

A small collection of the Emperor's vast harem of female companion spiders was lounged at his feet. They had been handpicked for the long trip to pleasure his every wish and need. They sat silent, wearing purple veils that covered their pretty faces.

As the beetle witnessed the strange sight at the back of the crate, he thought that he was having one of those dreams that always started with a capital D for danger, which was closely followed by an equally large A, N, G, E, and R, and all enclosed in big exclamation marks. The beetle was completely terrified.

The beetle's goose-pimples had goose-pimples. He tried to wriggle out of the web straps that had him secured firmly to a metal hip flask. He held his breath in anticipation of what was to come.

An unusual hush fell over the room deep down in the bottom of the boat. The only sound was the constant creaking of wood as the ship rocked gently back and forth on the waves.

'Hey... how are you feeling?'' The beetle heard a whispered voice from his right hand side.

The beetle could smell whoever owned the thick Irish accent before he could actually see him.

At first, the beetle struggled to move his neck because of the webbing straps, but he eventually managed to turned his head enough to see the battered and bruised face of the crab staring, googly-eyed, back at him.

'What's this all about?' the beetle asked.

He couldn't help but screw up his little face to try and stifle the smell wafting from the direction of the crab. The pong reminded the beetle of the time a huge slimy, smelly fishy thing had been washed up on the dockside. But the odour he could smell also had the pungent aroma of sweaty armpits.

'Beats me what's happening! I only came on the ship to borrow some toilet roll and they jumped me. I've tried to explain to this lot that it is friendly season and they were breaking the law... but they just grunted, covered me in web spit and marched off,' muttered the crab innocently.

'Smells like you been here a while.' The beetle didn't mean to offend, but his words raced out of his mouth before he realised what he was going to say.

'No... I've only been here since this morning,' the crab quickly added. 'Have you every tried to keep a shell nice and fresh? It's impossible!' The crab was obviously upset as he tried unsuccessfully to sniff his own armpits.

'Stop that talking,' bellowed Bollo loudly. He slapped the crab across the face.

The beetle turned back quickly, and on seeing the evil Emperor with the red eyes, he let out a shriek. The spider slithered slowly towards them.

When Balasz reached his destination he mouthed menacingly, 'I'm asking you again flat-face... Where is it?' Thankfully for the beetle, the question was directed at the crab. The words crawled out of the black spider's mouth. His accent was strong, and lacked any emotion or passion.

'I've told you before. I don't know what you are talking about,' the crab answered back bravely, just before a second slap from the muscular bodyguard spider connected solidly with his face.

'Look...sea creature, I'm Emperor Balasz... the one and only true ruler of the entire insect world... now tell me where the belt is?'

The crab spat a mouth full of blood at the feet of the tyrant and grunted, 'Look... Ball...hash, or whatever your name is, I don't know what you are talking about?'

'The name is Balasz.... Emperor Balasz.'

'That's what I said,' the crab replied, his thick Irish accent sailing away on the damp, salty air.

Emperor Balasz ignored the shell-fish's reply and turned to the beetle and asked him the same question. The beetle was scared stiff. He was shaking all over.

'I... I... I don't know what you mean.' The beetle answered. He knew another slap was coming from the bodyguard, but he was powerless to resist.

'You do know what I'm talking about, the 'Belt of Kings' Now where is the 'Belt of KKKIIINNNGSSS?' the words echoed around the underbelly of the boat, finally escaping out through the serving hatch.

'I don't know! I don't know what you are talking about!' The beetle started to cry. 'I'm from Ellesmere Port, near Liverpool; I'm only here for a two-week holiday visiting my aunty. I don't even know where she keeps the biscuits… never mind this 'Belt for the Kings' thing that you are on about.'

Emperor Balasz could feel a red storm bubbling up inside him, but he hid his feelings and cunningly released a playful grin instead. He started to stroke the beetle's protective shell. The beetle nervously smiled back, totally unaware of the anger that raged behind the Emperor's red eyes.

Emperor Balasz then turned sharply to Bollo, the big muscular spider and with a cold chilling voice, commanded as he pointed towards the beetle, 'Skin that new one. I want his hide as a cloak. And cut the claw off that ugly, fat, pink thing. Then throw what's left of the smelly creature back into the sea… where it belongs.'

'Hey! Who are you calling smelly?' the crab wailed loudly.

Emperor Balasz ignored the rant from the sea-creature and walked back to his private room. Without a second thought, the circle of killer spiders closed in around the helpless couple.

Chapter 4

'Under pier 14'

Later on, that same afternoon, down on the dockside, Bongo and his two mates headed for the centre of Tiger-Moth Bay with their instruments on their backs. Situated underneath pier 14, was the in-place to be seen and heard during Cree-season.

They found a spot opposite the drainpipe that spurted the giant people's sewage waste into the big, wet, blue thing. The water was turned into a strange muddy colour. As Bongo assembled his drums, he winced, as he regretfully recalled falling into that section of the big, wet, wild blue thing by the pipe when he was younger. Due to his little mishap he had developed whooping cough that soon lead to asthma, with which he had suffered ever since.

As the insect three-piece band set-up, Bongo looked about and was astonished to see how quickly the many different species of insects had entered the spirit of Cree-season. They had all stopped chasing each other about and trying to eat each other, and were now all getting on like a house on fire.

He found it quite amazing, as he observed how the middle-class centipedes were now out shopping for shoes, with their more working class cousins, the earwigs. Normally, they wouldn't be seen in the same street, never mind lacing up each others shoes in the same shop. But what tickled him most, was how the black ants and red ants, usually the most ferocious of enemies in wintertime, were now down on the sand, playing a game of mixed six-hundred-a-side football, using a wheat seed as the ball, and some small pebbles as goalposts. Bongo loved watching ants play football, because as soon as one of them kicked the ball, the other five-hundred and ninety-nine would form an orderly line, and follow behind.

A gang of industrious trapdoor spiders had kindly designed and installed a children's playground, with trampolines and swings, made from silk threads. Kiddie flies bounced along with the trapdoor spiders' own little children spiderlings, and the mothers sat on benches exchanging knitting patterns and tasty cooking recipes (but only of a vegetarian nature).

The sunny rays from the big, shiny, yellow thing were beating down with a vicious intensity which was relentless. The floor was sticky from the warmth and smelt of tar and salt from the sea. Every now and again, one of the giant people, up above on the pier, would drop some ice-cream that would seep through the floor boards and form pools in the sand. Insect children would come from miles to sample the delicious white substance.

'Are you ready?' Bongo yelled to his mates.

They nodded nervously.

He smiled as he shouted out, 'A one, a two,… a one, two, three, four!' His legs tapped a solid rhythm on the drum kit, which was quickly followed by his mate, Seamus, on double bass, and Malachy singing and strumming on guitar. The words from the homemade song sailed into the crowd.

> *'Cree-season and the weather is so easy,*
> *The big, shiny, yellow thing is sitting up in the big blue thing,*
> *Now all the insects are happy,*
> *And all the insects are dancing,*
> *What more can you say,*
> *About Sunnytime in Tiger-Moth Bay?'*

> *'Woke up this morning and I saw everyone smiling,*
> *There's no need to worry, or hurry, or even scurry away,*
> *Just told my Mama,*
> *That I'll be home in the morning,*
> *Cause I intend to stay…and play,*
> *Down in Tiger-Moth Bay'*

When the song had finished, the applause that filled the bay was more than generous. The band was overwhelmed.

Bongo loved all the attention that the group was receiving from the insects along the promenade. He knew, as a rule, that the majority of spiders were not great music lovers. They usually didn't like anything to do with things that made strange rhythm noises.

'The devil's music was invented by cockroaches,' his grandfather used to say, scornfully, whenever he ever heard anyone singing a song.

Spiders were more into hunting prey, making webs or scamper-dancing, which was a game that involved a spider running over a giant person's boot as many times as possible. It was extremely rare for a spider to actually sit down and listen to one of their own trying to display some latent talent by plucking any kind of musical device. In fact, it was frowned upon as unconventional and risky.

So it was a pleasure for Bongo and his mates to play to insects that really appreciated their musical efforts. He felt as though he was a thousand feet tall, as he looked around the many different types of bohemian faces that circled around them, tapping their feet, clapping their hands, or flapping their wings at the sounds that the band made.

Bongo then suddenly saw something that made his heart miss a beat. There, standing over by the empty apple barrel, staring at him with the most beautiful set of green eyes that he had ever seen, was a pretty, teenage female fly. He found himself staring unashamedly; she coyly smiled back at him but quickly looked away. Bongo appeared spellbound. He spun around on one leg and hit the drums with all his might. It was time to show off.

After three encores and an extra long drum solo, the spider group finished their set. Bongo wiped the sweat off his brow and looked across to where the girl of his dreams had been standing. But, sadly for Bongo, she had disappeared.

'Where did she go?' he asked the other two. His eyes wandered around like a horse galloping on a race track.

'Where's who gone?' Seamus replied, licking a grain of rice covered in ice-cream.

'That girl-fly. That girl-fly with the most dramatic, beautiful, exquisite green eyes that have ever sparkled in the night sky.'

'Looks he's off... old mister romantic!' Seamus roared.

Bongo threw his towel to his mates and ran off into the crowd, 'I'll be back in a couple of minutes.'

There were insects everywhere. The narrow streets were crowded with creatures of every shape, size and colour.

'I'll never see her again,' he sadly told himself.

He scampered up a drainpipe to try and get a better view.

Off in the distance, he saw the silhouette of a fly walking towards the cinema house which was showing a re-run of the insect's favourite movie

'The Earwig that came to dinner'. He pushed through the crowd, and gently tapped her on the wing.

'What do you want, darling?' an ageing blue-eyed bluebottle spun around and asked the young spider. 'I'm all yours for the right price!' the old fly let out a deafening cackle that proved to be a signal for a chorus of other insects to join in.

'Sorry... sorry... wrong coloured fly, with the wrong coloured mind,' Bongo answered back, and quickly rushed away.

Frantically, he continued his desperate search through the crowd, but the fly of his dreams was nowhere to be seen. He walked back to his mates, kicking his heels in temper. He was furious with himself for letting her get away. He reluctantly started to take his drums apart.

'That was very good,' Greeneyez the fly said to Bongo, as he sat on the ground undoing one of the drums.

He rose up too quickly, and banged his head on the bass drum.

'You are very talented,' she continued.

Bongo finally got to his eight feet.

'Hello... hello,' he struggled for the right words, 'I thought... I thought I'd lost you.' He wished he hadn't said that.

'Well... I didn't realise that I had been found.' She walked away before adding, 'I must be going.... before I'm lost again,' she laughed to herself and sauntered away, merrily swinging her purse.

'Go on… ask her out,' Seamus motioned to his starry eyed friend.

'I can't… what if she says no?'

'That's easy…. wrap her up in your web and tell her that you are going to eat her unless she says 'yes'. That's what I always do,' Seamus offered his priceless piece of advice.

The other two stared at the bass player.

'When was the last time you went out with someone?' Bongo asked Seamus.

'Two years, eight months, three weeks, sixteen days and a couple of hours… to the exact day!'

'No wonder! And it will probably be another two years, eight months, three weeks, sixteen days and a couple of hours… to the exact day, before you go out with someone else.' Bongo and Malachy laughed out aloud.

But Bongo knew his friend was certainly right about asking her out before it was too late.

He sprinted after the fly. He ducked and dived amongst the crowd and eventually popped up in front of her and asked nervously, 'I was wondering if you would like to … to ….to….' Bongo struggled with the words. His tongue was all tied and stuck to the roof of his mouth.

'I would love to,' Greeneyez finished the sentence for him. Her eyelashes fluttered slowly, Bongo's heart melted, and then broke in two.

'Great… I'll pick you up tomorrow.' As he trotted away he added, 'What do you like to do?'

'Fly about, regurgitate my food, eat it again and then have fun rolling about in horse manure.' She could see the confusion (and disgust) on his face. She laughed 'Sorry… I was messing with you. It's up to you… I really don't mind.' She strolled away, still giggling to herself.

Bongo literally floated back to his mates and the three friends packed up their stuff. They headed to the sands for an afternoon of sunbathing and playing regimental football with the ants.

Chapter 5

'Nut-cracker suite'

Back on board the banana boat, the atmosphere bordered on the hostile, with a strong hint of fear. Emperor Balasz glanced into the full length mirror, and admired his new beetle-cloak that had been presented to him earlier that day.

He loved the strange texture of the material as soon as he had wrapped it around his thin body. He wished deep down that it could have been just a couple of shades blacker, and maybe a little longer, so it would swish as he swirled into a room.

His loyal lieutenants had all been summoned to the war room that was temporarily housed inside a large empty barrel. They sat facing each other on a round table that had been assembled from several old metal coins.

There was the usual silence.

No one in the room would ever contemplate uttering a single syllable until the Emperor had spoken first.

'What are you doing to get me MY BELT?' Balasz's voice danced menacingly from his mouth, as his evil glare burnt into the spider that had the unfortunate title of 'The Commander for Finding Things.'

'Sorry Emperor… but we haven't found it yet,' the 'Commander for Finding Things' announced. A slight tremor shook his voice.

'Well, I can bloody well see that.' There was no humour in the Emperor's reply.

'But it's only a matter of time your Highness…. Trust me! We will locate it soon.'

Emperor Balasz slammed his thin, spindly fist down hard onto the metal table. 'I haven't got the time… I want the belt now. I'm due to moult my ninth and final skin in a few days…. and I need that belt to save me.' A tiny piece of flaked skin came away from his far left leg.

In the background, standing by the little round entrance, Bollo, the muscular spider, had been waiting. He walked menacingly towards the table. The giant claw, which had been viciously snapped off the crab earlier that afternoon (and thoroughly washed and soaked in rose petal oil), was held firmly in his grasp.

'But…but… but Emperor, I've done the best I could.' the 'Commander for Finding Things' continued nervously, wriggling about in his seat. 'I've despatched our top scouts to all corners of the docks… but no-one will tell us anything. They all go into their shells, or cob-webs, when we ask them about the belt.'

'Have you tried to apply some pressure on those peasants?' As Balasz spoke, he slyly nodded towards his loyal bodyguard, who was now positioned directly behind the stuttering spider.

'But it's different here, Emperor Balasz. All the insects seem to get on with each other.... they are very friendly. Some even gave us some fine homemade cake.'

'Cake... cake! I'm falling to bits before your very eyes, and you are going ashore to munch on some titbits!'

That was the last straw. He signalled to Bollo, the muscular spider who clamped the unfortunate 'Commander for Finding Things' around the head with the teeth of the crabs claw.

He picked the spider up with the shell. The 'Commander for Finding Things' eight legs' kicked out wildly. His antennae flapped around like a mouse's hind legs caught in a trap. All the other spiders around the round table looked on in horror. No one moved a muscle. No one went to help the poor Commander.

'Now, what were you saying?' Balasz spat out the words, 'perhaps we need to apply just a little more pressure... to show these insects who's boss. Is that what you are trying to say?' The Emperor moved close. His face was only inches away from his victim. 'Well, I agree. You heard him, Bollo.'

He motioned to the bodyguard again. 'He's telling you to apply some more pressure.'

The 'Commander of Finding Things' tried to speak, but nothing came out.

The muscular spider squeezed the device in his huge legs. The claw tightened a notch or two. The 'Commander for Finding Things' eyes' bulged and swelled. He tried in vain to grab the claw off the muscular spider. He let out a strained 'Urrrrghh' followed by an 'Arrrrgh' that escaped from deep inside his throat.

Suddenly, and to everyone's surprise, the 'Commander for Finding Things' head popped, like a Christmas walnut being squeezed in a nut cracker. There was a stunned silence throughout the room.

'I bet he won't be finding things anymore,' Emperor Balasz laughed out loud. The noise echoed around the room, even the ship stopped rocking and rolling on the tide.

After an uncomfortable interval, the rest of the spiders nervously joined in the laughter. Unfortunately, most of them were also busy wiping sticky blood and spider brains off their uniforms.

The Emperor's face immediately became serious again. The laughter duly stopped, and all sets of eyes stared firmly at the floor. He turned to the 'First Lady Minister in Charge of Making Pretty but Functional Webs' and told her that she had just been promoted to the highly prestigious, and highly dangerous (and often mind-blowing) position of 'The First Lady Commander for Finding Things', and her first duty was to find the 'Belt of Kings,' and quickly. He also instructed her to find a large palace fit for an Emperor. He was sick to death of being cooped up in this wooden, rocking coffin, especially with this bunch of cake-eating, no-good, hairy-legged, useless idiots.

'You'd better not let me down,' he added sharply.

'I won't Emperor Balasz... I'll find it... I'll find the 'Belt of Kings'... you can be sure of that,' she said confidently.

She stared across at the muscular bodyguard, cleaning the fresh blood off the crab claw. By his feet, the headless, but multi-legged body of the ex-'Commander for Finding Things' lay twitching on the floor.

Emperor Balasz waltzed out of the room with his new beetle-cloak trailing behind him. He could feel his bones getting old and his skin getting saggier, looser, and flakier. He summoned his servants to crack open a fresh coconut so he could relax in a nice bath of coconut milk, and soak his aching body.

Anthony Bunko

Chapter 6

'Entering Buzztown'

Duggan the rat lowered his long snout to the ground and allowed his freshly washed, and smartly dressed, passenger to hop off. Bongo's feet touched the floor, a petal leaf clutched firmly in his grasp.

'Wait here Duggan. I won't be long,' Bongo instructed his carriage for the night.

'OK,' Duggan replied, 'but you'd better hurry up… my uncle has booked me to take a family of French snails on a tour of the quayside this evening.'

Bongo straightened up his waistcoat and repositioned his lucky hat. He swallowed hard as he stared at the well-lit blue, neon sign that flashed above the archway.

It displayed three simple words:-

'Welcome to Buzztown.'

Underneath, smaller letters stated *'All poisonous fangs and web holders to be left at the entrance. This is a peaceful place. This is fly country.'*

Bongo took a deep breath and strolled in.

'It may be a peaceful place,' he thought, 'but it don't half pong!' He wondered how on earth flies chose to live in such smelly surroundings.

The place was positioned in the middle of a rubbish tip. Rotten food and animal droppings littered the pavements.

As the young spider walked further into the fly-city, he could feel hundreds of sets of coloured eyes staring at his every movement. He could just make them out, glistening in the shadows of the darkness.

He found himself whispering. 'It could be worse; Greeneyez could have been a butterfly'. He knew that they were a real tough old breed of insect. On the outside they looked all sweetness and light, but underneath those colourful wings, and playful smiles, lay a very nasty breed of creepy-crawly. They would bite the head off a baby worm without thinking twice, and they didn't like outsiders one bit... not even in Cree-season.

'What's he doing here?' way off in the shadows Bongo overheard someone asking. He instantly knew that the comment was aimed at him.

'Go back to your own kind... spider-boy!' another fly shouted aggressively at the handsome teenager.

An object, thrown from a chink in the wall, hit his shoulder. He turned quickly, but nothing else stirred in the darkness.

He shuffled on, determined not to be intimidated. He checked the address on the piece of paper that Greeneyez had given to him.

'Number 76, Legless Spider Lane'

'Very funny!' he thought. He didn't know if it was her sense of humour or actually the name of the real street.

He looked up to see what the street he was in was called. It was 'Soft belly Beetle Place'. He shook his head. Next on the route was 'Six Feet Only Woodlice Way.' He knew that flies were the jokers of the insect world, but they were lucky his brother wasn't here; he would have ripped every sign off the wall and bashed a couple of heads with them; Cree-season or not.

At last, he found what he was looking for. He stood in front of the door and finally built up enough courage to gently knock. Several moments later, an older, but extremely attractive woman-fly opened the door. She was bottle feeding six, or seven maggots, that wriggled about in her arms.

Bongo rightly assumed that the woman-fly, with the babies, must be the mother of the house.

She looked nervous and asked, 'Can... can ... I help you... young spider?'

'Is Greeneyez in?' Bongo politely replied.

He could instantly see a very strong family resemblance. Bluebottles with green eyes were very rare indeed, so to see two, living in the same house was almost unheard of.

He could also see an uncomfortable look of confusion spreading on her face.

'Its OK Mam... he's here for me,' Greeneyez said, skipping out of the front door and grabbing one of Bongo's legs, as she went past. She was wearing a beautiful, and revealing, red and white summer dress. She was dressed to impress her new spider boyfriend.

'I'll be back before ten... unless, of course, he's eaten me by then,' she laughed sarcastically.

In panic, Bongo looked directly at the mother and shook his head in innocence.

'I wouldn't do that. I've never liked the taste of bluebottle,' he lied. He could feel himself flushing red in his cheeks.

The two teenagers' walked back towards the archway. They passed the prying eyes, with loose tongues, hiding in the shadows. Bongo heard someone make a comment about mixed insect relationships, but Greeneyez was more than a match for the faceless insect with her cutting reply. She wished that flies' wouldn't be so small-minded when it came to things like that. It embarrassed her, and it made her so ashamed to be one of them.

They reached the archway, and Greeneyez broke the silence, as she asked, 'Where are you taking me then... incey wincey.... spiderrrrrrr?' She joked again. 'I hope it's somewhere nice... I'm absolutely starving. I could eat the big toe off a wild bull.'

'Yeah…. somewhere very special,' Bongo lied yet again.

He wondered where the hell they were going to go on their first date. He had been so excited about taking her out, that, although he had remembered to have a wash, borrowed his older brother's aftershave, and arranged the transport, he had completely forgotten about the most important thing. Where was he going to take her?

'Yeah, somewhere grand!' and he quickly added, 'but I need to go and see my Uncle Paddy first. Oh! And hey less of the incey wincey spiderrrr thing, or I will eat you.' He smiled.

She innocently fluttered her eyelashes. Bongo was in love for the first time in his spider life.

'Are you going to take me ballooning?' she cried excitedly.

She had always dreamt of grabbing hold of a handsome young spider's back, as they 'ballooned' romantically between objects, using his silk web as a line like Tarzan and Jane in those old movies.

There was a hint of sadness and pain in Bongo reply, 'Well… not quite…..ballooning.'

To be truthful, his last experience of ballooning had seen him fall from a great height while trying to swing between his house and a green-glass bottle. He had landed heavily, fracturing his knee cap on his third left leg from the front.

'But, wherever we end up, we are going to travel in style.' He quickly added, as his loud whistle sailed out into the darkness, looking to capture someone's attention.

Suddenly, out popped Duggan munching on a rotten carrot, and, at the same time picking his nose. Bongo glared at his uncouth friend in utter disgust.

'Howdy... Miss Fly.... My name is Duggan. Bongo's told me all about you. I've been looking around for some horse manure for you to roll in,' the rat joked, much to the annoyance of the spider, who glared at the rodent so coldly that Duggan could have turned into a snow-rat in the middle of sunnytime.

The two young insects scrambled onto the back of the rat taxi. Bongo carefully helped his new girl-fly up.

Before they had a chance to get comfortable, Duggan had decided to become fully involved in the conversation. He squealed happily, 'Ask me who I am going out with then.... go on...it's not just you kids that can fall in love. Go on... ask me!'

Bongo felt ashamed; this was turning out to be a nightmare. If his legs had been long enough he would have stretched them around his mate's neck and proceeded to strangle him on the spot. He now really wished he had walked instead of asking Duggan to do him a favour.

He nudged Greeneyez to indicate to her to just ignore the rat, but it was too late. Greeneyez' question had already left her mouth before Bongo had time to stop her.

'Who are you going out with then handsome Mr Duggan?' she asked.

'Hasn't he told you?' he sneered at Bongo, then continued, 'Well, if you must know, I'm going out with a rat princess. Her father was the chief of a rat colony that lived underneath a village in Zambolo. That's in Africa.'

Before the rat could finish his explanation, Greeneyez jumped back in and commented jokingly, 'Is he the one with the massive Elephant bone in his nose?'

Bongo glanced at her in disbelief and asked, 'Have you seen him?'

'No,' she giggled. 'Of course I haven't seen him. I thought it was a joke... a myth you know. Like the one about the fast slow-worm, or the centipede with no toes.'

'Or the black earwig!' Bongo joined in.

Both insects cried with laughter.

Their rodent mode of transport came to a screeching halt. His passengers nearly become dislodged from their seat.

'It's no joke, young lady, it's no joke at all.' Duggan was cross and upset, his whiskers twitching. He roared, 'He was the chief of a rat colony that lived under a village in Zambolo. And by the way, it's not an elephant bone in his snout... it's a real zebra bone... so there!'

Everyone went quiet as Duggan turned and trotted off in a huff. He began to mutter to himself.

The two youngsters perched on his back, secretly giggled and nudged each other.

After travelling several blocks, and luckily surviving a life-threatening close shave with a tram, which fortunately Duggan avoided at the last minute, they finally arrived at their first intended destination.

Bongo, and his gorgeous companion, disembarked off their mount. They walked quietly hand-in-leg into the secret vault, where the spider's Uncle Paddy worked.

The vault was hidden across the street from the 'Upside down fishing boat' palace where the mayor lived. The secret and safe place was full of insect memorabilia which had been found, lost, or pinched down the years from the giant people.

Along the far wall there hung hand-painted portraits of all the past insect mayors. The couple glanced up at the canvas of the first ever mayor of Tiger-Moth Bay, Brendan the Eccentric Earwig. Brendan was famous for inventing insect line-dancing and ration books.

The pair strolled on.

Sixty-five portraits later, there staring down at them was the comical image of Terry the bilingual Woodlouse. He had the honour of being the current mayor. Up to this point he hadn't been famous for inventing anything except adding rule 3 to the great Cree-season treaty of Dublin.

In the centre of the room stood an oil lamp that had been washed ashore many moons ago. Inside the glass section of the lamp was an object, so shiny, so beautiful that it took Greeneyez's breath away.

'Is that the 'Belt of Kings?' Greeneyez asked in total awe. The respect was evident in the shaky tone of her voice.

Flies were rarely, if ever, allowed into this purely spider-dominated place at any time, even during the Cree-season. She marvelled at the beauty of the object in the glass case. It enthralled her. She was spellbound as she fell in love with the famous 'Belt of Kings.'

What the insect didn't know was that the 'Belt of Kings' was not a belt at all. It was, in fact, a floral pink tourmaline ring, decorated in an intricate petal design, set in white gold and topped with a gleaming pink stone. The ring had been lost by some rich giant person a long, long time ago. The lady giant, who once owned the ring, had accidentally dropped it through the slats on the pier. And there it had stayed ever since, in the safe, but grubby mitts of the Dublin creepy-crawlies.

'Yes it is the 'Belt of Kings',' Bongo replied, rather smugly.

'I've heard so much about it,' she said, before adding excitedly, 'I've heard that it can make an insect invisible just by looking at it. And I've been told that insects can grow fifty times their normal size just by touching it and saying some magical words.'

'Really!' Bongo said casually and rather coyly.

She rushed up closer to take a better look, pressing her pretty face up close against the glass. 'Oh yeah, and did you hear about the centipede that grew to the size of an elephant and squashed a hundred giants that stood in its path.'

Well, Bongo had heard many rumours and myths about the famous Dublin 'Belt of Kings'. Apparently, it had first come to prominence during the reign of King Fergal, the great white-haired spider of Ireland, during the conflicts with the Spanish caterpillars. Legend had it that the long, green, hairy, foreign insects had turned up in their own armada with the intention of raiding, pillaging and turning all the Irish insects into slithering vegetarians.

Bongo sat Greeneyez down and told her all about King Fergal and the war with the caterpillars and how, as the story goes, the King had two of his front legs chopped off by a caterpillar with a razor sharp pineapple shoot. The legend stated that the King hobbled to where the 'Belt' was kept and rubbed it over his body. The next day he grew some more limbs, which were double in number and made him stronger by the power of ten.

Allegedly, the army of Spanish caterpillars upon witnessing this, fled back home. They instantly spread a rumour about how this King-guy had had all his legs ripped off, his eyes plucked out, but then had grown them all back like a flower growing summer petals. The Spanish caterpillars never ventured back, and rumour had it that the entire breed retired to one cactus bush near Barcelona.

How true the story of the King and the caterpillars was, no-one really knew. But Bongo knew that insects' loved to conjure up rumours, just as much as flies love to spread germs. So, down the years, the stories had grown larger, and spread further and wider throughout the land. Eventually all the insects knew (and had probably added a few more lines to the stories themselves just to help it on its way) about the magical powers of the legendary 'Belt of Kings'.

Bongo's favourite was the one about how King Fergal had slain a giant who had tried to take the 'Belt' out of its sacred resting place.

Again Bongo didn't really know if there was an ounce of truth in the tale, but as they were growing up, when they were told it, it made him, and his pals, feel good inside.

In all that time Bongo hadn't heard the one about the 'Belt of Kings' turning insects invisible, or helping a centipede grow to the size of an elephant, and go stamping giants into the ground. But it was a fairly good tale that he would share with his mates later on.

Insect Kings were eventually abolished in Dublin at the turn of the century, along with slavery and deporting criminal insects to Australia, but the tradition of the 'Belt' continued to this very day.

If there was an issue down in the bay, however big or very big (you see insects never have small problems, it's something to do with their size) the insect council would rub the 'Belt' to make the issue go away. Sometimes rubbing the belt worked, sometimes it didn't, but whatever the outcome, the 'Belt' was never wrong. Even if the issue of the day didn't actually disappear, the insects always blamed something, or someone else.

'But why are we here?' Greeneyez found herself whispering quietly, out of a mark of respect.

'Well, my Uncle Paddy 'O' Dacey, is the official guardian of the 'Belt of Kings',' Bongo said proudly, before adding with greater pride, 'you see no one will ever pinch the 'Belt' with my Uncle looking after it,' Bongo informed her. His eyes searched around the large vault for a sign of his old uncle's whereabouts.

'He was once the 'Heavyweight Insect Champion' of the entire world,' he added. 'He knocked out the previously undefeated, legendary champion, Gizzy-the-Grasshopper, in the eighth round. You must have heard about the 'Rumble in the Junkyard.'

Bongo yelled out his name, and looked around to see where the hell his uncle could be. He began to worry.

'Perhaps... someone has stolen him instead of the 'Belt',' sniggered Greeneyez.

'Oh! Very funny. No, he's probably in hiding, looking at us as we speak. Just watch this.' He put his hand on the glass case, fully expecting the old daddy long legs to pounce from his hide-out.

But still nothing stirred.

Then, off in the distance, the pair could make out a noise that sounded like thunder cracking in the big blue thing that the birds flew in. But it was much too close, and to regular for that.

The youngsters wandered over to the corner of the vault where the noise was coming from. It didn't take them long to discover what had been behind the loud sound. There, flat out on the floor behind the desk, sleeping like a baby and snoring like a terminally ill warthog, was none other than Bongo's great Uncle Paddy 'O' Dacey.

'Uncle Paddy…. Uncle Paddy,' Bongo yelled.

'Ready to pounce like a tiger!' Greeneyez said sarcastically. She was enjoying this.

There was no movement from the unconscious spider. Greeneyez spotted a glass of rain water on the desk. 'This should wake him up,' she said, as she threw the contents of the glass all over the well-built daddy long-legs.

'What! What round is it…?' Uncle Paddy sprang automatically to his feet and started shadow boxing with himself. 'Am I winning? Am I cut?' he continued in some sort of trance. 'Give me my gum shield in….I'm going back in!'

'No Uncle Patrick…. remember, you don't fight anymore. Well, not since that money spider knocked you out the last time.'

'That was a fluky punch,' Uncle Paddy replied defensively, after finally realising where he was.

'Uncle Paddy… you are supposed to be guarding the 'Belt of Kings', not falling asleep behind a desk,' Bongo said, accidentally kicking over a small gin bottle that lay half-empty on the floor under the table. 'What's this Uncle? You know what the doctor told you about drinking the giant men's brew.'

'It's just for the company… my boy; it's just for the company. It's so lonely in this job.'

As the old street fighting spider dipped his head in a bucket of rain water and cracked his knuckles, Greeneyez could see that he must have been a very intimidating figure in his time. He was as wide as he was tall, with legs like tree trunks, and a flat, squashed nose on a battled hardened face.

'How do you do, Mister Paddy 'O' Dacey?' Greeneyez held out her tiny hands, which were dwarfed by the massive right leg of the spider.

'Feel that.' Uncle Paddy clenched his muscles. 'If you get hit with that… you are not getting back up.'

Greeneyez moved away sharply. Panic replaced the smile on her face.

'Sorry… sorry I didn't mean you… my dear… I would never hit a lady…..' Uncle Paddy blushed while apologising profusely.

He took a swig out of the gin bottle, then marshalled Bongo, his nephew, to one side and whispered quietly in his ear, 'Hey! My boy, can I have a quick word?'

'Yes, of course, Uncle Paddy,' Bongo chuckled, and waved at Greeneyez.

'Are you still a spider?' The ex-street fighter had a serious look on his face.

The teenager nodded, unsure quite where this line of questioning was leading too.

'You haven't been to one of those brainwashing insect cult, have you my boy? 'Cause if you have been messing with that lot, I'll beat you with my leather belt.'

'Don't be so stupid, Uncle.'

'Well, am I still drunk then?' the old street fighter slurred.

'Probably...but why do you ask Uncle? What's the problem? What are you trying to say?'

They both looked over towards Greeneyez who stood by the oil lamp, still mesmerised by the 'Belt'.

'Look my boy, I realise that she is extremely beautiful,' Uncle Paddy continued.

Bongo smiled proudly to himself. He knew she was beautiful and more importantly she was with him.

Uncle Paddy edged in closer. 'But ain't she a bit too much of a .... fly... for you?'

'A what.... a fly?' Bongo raised his voice.

'Sshhh,' his uncle tried to put his legs over the youngster's mouth. 'Haven't you noticed her wings and those big green eyes? Although I'm still a little plastered, I can tell you now that she ain't no spider. I've travelled about, and unfortunately they don't make lady spiders as gorgeous as that.'

Bongo laughed. He finally realised why his Uncle was acting so strange. 'But it's Cree-season, Uncle Paddy… its Cree-season. She's my girl-fly.'

'Is it?.... Is it really Cree-season? I didn't realise. Well, that's OK then.' He put his legs over Bongo's shoulders and they scuttled back to the fly.

'Everything OK?' asked Greeneyez.

'Everything is great, my girl,' Uncle Paddy replied, before adding, 'hells bells…if its Cree-season, I must apologise to the cockroach that I punched on my way to work this morning. He must think I'm a right bully-longlegs!'

There was a pause, while someone tried to think of what to say next.

'But why did you punch him Mister 'O' Dacey?' Yet again Greeneyez appeared shocked.

'He was whistling out of tune.'

The fly glanced worriedly towards Bongo.

After a time of formal conversation, and an embarrassing demonstration by Uncle Paddy who insisted that he showed Greeneyez how he had knocked out Gizzy the Grasshopper, Bongo decided to get to the main reason for the stop-off visit.

'We have got to go now, Uncle Paddy… but my Mam asked if you would like to come around for tea on Sunday,' he quickly added, 'but she told me to warn you not to turn up drunk, and no picking fights with the Murphy clan next door.'

'You're mother has always had a thing about us insects enjoying ourselves. She would never let your poor late father have any fun, rest his spider soul. He was always working in the garden, or doing work on that boot. She's an old sour-puss. Now tell her I'll be there and I will behave perfectly.' He smiled mischievously.

Greeneyez noticed that the old spider's fangs were missing. Probably knocked out in some illegal street brawl, she imagined.

Bongo waved goodbye, knowing full well that come Sunday, Uncle Paddy 'O' Dacey would stagger up to their boot, two hours late, half-cut and itching to punch someone.

'You can take the daddy long-legs out of the gutter, but you can't take the gutter out of the daddy long-legs,' thought Bongo, watching his uncle waddle ungracefully back towards the desk.

Uncle Paddy settled back into his comfortable chair, criss-crossed his legs on the desk and was sound asleep before the youngsters' had left the building.

Outside, Duggan was pacing back and forth nervously. 'Where have you been Bongo? You know I've got to take those French snails on that tour of the dockside. Hurry up…. where do you wanna go, anyway?'

Bongo whispered in his ear, so that his partner couldn't make out what he was saying, and said, 'I don't know. She wants to go somewhere special, and she's starving. So just run around, until I think of something.'

Greeneyez was still feeling bad about taking the mickey out of Duggan and his unbelievably tale of the African Princess and her father, who had a real zebra bone in his nose. So, during their journey, she decided to try and make amends. She asked him how he had lost his tail. Bongo was too slow to stop her. He gently kicked her leg, trying to get her to change the subject, but Duggan was already off like a racehorse out of the stalls, that had found itself in a 'Whoever ends up last will be packed off to the slaughterhouse' Grand National.

'I thought you'd never ask.' The rat turned his head around, while still continuing to race along blindly between the pavement and the boots of the giant people. He added proudly, 'Have you ever heard the story about the hero of the Iron monger's scrap?'

'I... I think I have,' she lied and glared at Bongo for assistance.

'That hero was me.' His face beamed.

Bongo put his eyes in his legs and cursed his luck.

Greeneyez on the other hand, had only ever met one hero in the past. That was a male fly called Flappy, who had single-handedly rescued a party of school flies that had fallen into a bowl of porridge, while out on a field trip.

Duggan yelled, 'Twelve days and fourteen nights we fought….like cat and dog…it was….'

'Or cat and rat,' she joked.

'I didn't think of that.' Duggan repeated the story, changing it ever so slightly. 'Fourteen days and sixteen nights … we fought.'

Greeneyez stared at Bongo. The spider just shook his head in an 'I told you not to ask him' sort of way, as the rat added 'It was like cat and rat...it was. But, although I crawled from that alleyway bruised and battered, but victorious with fourteen cat scalps in my belt, my tail was lost forever.... but the good thing was.....'

Suddenly there was a loud bang as Duggan crashed headfirst into something soft that was blocking their route. The passengers and driver went flying but all landed safe and sound in the sand next to the offending roadblock.

'Sorry about that,' Duggan shook his head. 'I travel this way all the time and I don't remember ever bumping into something here before.'

'What is it?' Greeneyez finally asked, wiping sand out of her large eyes.

Bongo raced around excitedly for a better look. He reappeared in near hysterics. 'It can't be.... It is.... It is!'

'What is it?' the other two shouted.

The rat and fly skittered up to the big grey object and sniffed it. They were still none the wiser.

'It's a dead giant.' Bongo answered them, before adding, 'and it's still quite warm.'

'Are you sure?' asked Duggan suspiciously.

'Yes...I know what a dead giant looks like, and it looks like that.' His little toes pointed towards the road block.

'But how do you know it's dead?' Greeneyez asked. 'Perhaps it's just sleeping or hung-over from drinking too much of that dark liquid… a bit like your Uncle Paddy!'

Bongo ignored the cutting comment about his family and said, 'Because of this.' He held up his blood soaked pads. 'It appears that its throat has been cut from ear to ear.'

The rodent stepped back in disgust.

On the other hand, Greeneyez stepped forward and licked her lips. 'I haven't tasted real human blood for ages.' She flew up to find a better spot.

Bongo turned to his vermin mate. 'Duggan… do us a big favour. Don't tell anyone about us finding this body for a while…please…I'll owe you one.'

Duggan nodded unconvincingly, and trotted away. Bongo was also famished. He clambered up the giant's ice-cold expressionless face, where he found Greeneyez sucking the red juices up with her feelers.

Chapter 7

'On the frozen playground'

Bongo estimated that they didn't have long alone on the dead giant person before Duggan blabbed to someone. The spider realised that the rat's jaw was as slack as a ships main sail flapping about in a gale on the Irish Sea.

The only saving grace for the teenage couple was that Duggan had told so many lies in his life, that it would take him quite a while to convince anyone he was telling the truth.

But Bongo knew that they would eventually come, so he had to make the most of this unexpected stroke of good fortune.

The two teenagers frolicked in the open wound that split the giant's throat in half. They greedily feasted on the raw meat until their bellies were full to bursting point. Greeneyez looked like she had applied lipstick, quite badly, around her mouth. Her little face was covered in the human's blood.

After a much needed lunch, they both relaxed on the frozen and exposed big toes of the deceased.

Unknown to the two insects, the reason the giant person was bootless, was because they had been stolen, along with his wallet, three gold teeth, and a one-way ticket to a brand new life in a city called New York.

'Let's go and explore some more!' Greeneyez beckoned towards the spider, who had actually started to doze off on the comfortable digits of the giant.

Bongo jumped to his feet.

He peered up the trouser leg of the stiff and said, 'OK…. I'll tell you what? Let's have a race up the legs of this giant, and the first to reach the little pocket on its waist coat with that red handkerchief in it is the winner.'

Greeneyez scrabbled back up the giant's toe to get a better look, and to see the size of the task. She spotted the finish line way off in the distance. She hopped back down and nodded in agreement to the challenge.

The two insects crouched down in starting positions. There was a serious expressions covering their faces.

'Are you ready?…. steady?..' but before he continued Greeneyez interrupted.

'Oh… incey, wincey spiderrrrr, are you sure you are up for this?' she teased.

'Up for it… I'll show you, Bongo roared, 'Are you ready?… steady?…. GO!' He sprinted up the left leg, rushing passed the shin-bone, and heading towards the knee-cap.

What he didn't know was that Greeneyez had pretended to run up the other leg, but had slyly stopped when she saw the spider disappear up the material of the grey trousers. She knew that a fly could never beat a young healthy spider in a foot race. So she had no intention of trying to play fair.

So, while poor Bongo ducked and dived his way to the finish line, she used her God-given wings instead, and flew straight up to the prearranged meeting point.

When Bongo finally reached the pocket in the waist coat, the smile dropped off his face. His new girl-fly was lying out on the red handkerchief, pretending to sunbathe.

He was panting and puffing; sweat dripping off his brow. He kicked out at a button with one of his feet in disgust.

'I thought you eight-legged creatures were supposed to be fast!' Greeneyez smiled smugly at him.

Bongo was lost for words. He realised he wouldn't live this down if his mates ever found out about it. It was bad enough if they knew he had been beaten in a race by another breed of insect, but it would be criminal if they knew that the winner of the foot-race was not only a fly, but a girl-fly, who lived in a street named 'Legless Spider Place.'

'Let's do it again,' he demanded forcefully, the knuckles of his legs white with rage.

Greeneyez agreed, keeping her smile well hidden.

They lined up again using the giant's overgrown toesnails as the starting post. This time, Bongo ran as fast as the wind. He took several shortcuts as he sprinted up the cold, and hairy limbs of the giant person.

But, as before, when he reached the finish line, Greeneyez was again sitting there. This time she was pretending to be asleep. She could see by the young spider's sullen demeanour, how upset he was. He head butted the dead giant's chest, which made him dizzy.

She had heard how dull spiders could be, but hadn't really believed the stories her father had told her. 'No creatures could be that stupid,' she thought, but Bongo had just proved the point…not once, but twice!

She declined the offer of a 'winner takes all' third, and final race, instead insisting that they should go and explore the caves on the north face of the giant instead.

Bongo reluctantly agreed.

His shoulders were hunched in defeat as they both climbed up onto the rugged face of the giant.

The giant's lips were blue from death and firmly shut. Bongo used all of his strength in his legs to prise open the entrance to the mouth cave. It creaked and crocked, then eventually opened. They wriggled on their bellies to get inside. Bongo positioned a piece of driftwood between the lifeless lips, like a wooden prop used to hold up the roof of a coalmine.

Once inside, Greeneyez sat on the ivory teeth, that were more green than white. The interior was dark, and smelt of decay, mixed with beer in equal measure.

Bongo struck a match across the teeth. The cave was suddenly illuminated. They were pleasantly surprisingly at how warm it was inside the dark cavern.

'Hope there's none of them little nit-things in here,' Bongo said. 'They really give me the willies.'

'I thought that spiders weren't afraid of anything?' Greeneyez's reply was fast

'No, not true. Spiders hate lots of things.' She could see a physical shiver dance up his spine. He continued, 'we hate water; fire, other insects beating us at races,' he was still upset, 'cats and especially head lice. Those nits are really nasty. They never give in during a fight.'

She was dying to say something, but she decided to decline.

They both spent several moments cautiously investigated the interior of the cave. Greeneyez had decided to stick close to him. When they were satisfied that they were alone, they started to act and play like normal insect teenagers. It was as though they had found themselves in a shop made from sugar candy on Christmas morning.

They ran around, shouting and screaming. They bounced up and down on the inflated, pink tongue of the giant, which had obviously spoken its last words. They laughed aloud, the sound echoing around the inside of the mouth.

Bongo was looking for an opportunity to make up for his poor showing in the foot-race with the fly, so he started to show off. He went through a routine of back-flips and forward rolls, but unfortunately he bounced so hard, he tumbled backward, falling down the black hole at the back of the cave.

Greeneyez was helpless with laughter. She giggled until her sides hurt. After she managed to contain herself enough, she ambled over to see if her boy-spider was alright.

'Are you there?' Greeneyez yelled down the dark passage.

Her jolly expression turned to concern, when the only sound to come back to greet her was the wind rushing back up the dark tunnel.

She leant further over the hole to get a better view. Her large eyes squinted in the darkness, as she held onto the giant's tonsils for support.

Suddenly, she felt a tap on her shoulder from behind. This made her jump so high she banged her head on the soft roof of the cave.

'You frightened the life out of me,' she shouted angrily at Bongo, who had miraculously reappeared and was standing behind her. 'Well; how… how did you do that?' She punched him in the chest. He smiled.

'I slid down that tunnel and luckily for me, I popped out through the section of the throat that had been sliced open. Otherwise, I could have been lost way down in his stomach. I did scrape all my knees on the giant's chest hair.' He showed her his glazed kneecaps, hoping for a flicker of sympathy from the upset fly.

He could see by her body language that the fly was not amused. The ends of her wings were twitching manically, which was never a good sign. Normally in the world of flies (or any insect with wings) this indicated that something (or someone) was bugging them big time.

He gave her a while to cool down before mentioning that he had another great idea.

'Another great idea; I don't remember you having the first one yet!' Greeneyez snapped back. Now it was her turn to be in a mood.

'OK… I have an idea…. quick; follow me.' He grabbed her hand, and they climbed upwards to the back of the cave towards the nostrils.

Once there, they found two, tightly packed tunnels. Greeneyez could see daylight at the end of one of them.

'Come on; let's go…' Bongo said, climbing into one of the shoots.

'I'm not sliding down there… I'll ruin my dress,' she replied, 'what's all that green sticky stuff?'

'Come on… it will be great.'

Before she had time to argue, the young spider pushed himself down. He sailed through the human slide, shooting out the other end, landing just above the blue-coloured lips.

Now the fly had a choice to make. It was either follow the handsome (but slightly irritating), spider down the tunnel, and risk ruining her dress in the green stuff, or stand all alone inside the head of a dead giant.

It wasn't really much of a choice.

She tucked her wings in as tight as she could, and reluctantly followed her companion. She shot out of the other end like a bullet fired from a gun. She crashed into Bongo. They both became entangled, rolling down passed the mouth cave, over the chin, skipping over the throat and landed with a bump on the giant's large belly.

Bongo accidentally found himself positioned on top of the fly.

'Sorry… sorry,' she panted, laughing at the same time, 'but you should have seen your face.'

Although slightly dazed, he also saw the funny side of the situation.

'That was great,' she said, 'let's do it again!'

Bongo looked into her eyes. They were glistening like two twinkling stars in the big blue thing that turned into the big black thing during the time when they slept.

Bongo's heart beat faster.

He could smell her breath. His lips moved closer. He couldn't stop himself. They were moving by themselves. He tried to retrieve them but they seemed to have a mind of their own. They edged closer to the girl-fly. The only audible noise was the beating of their young hearts.

Bongo felt strange. He felt all peculiar.

Greeneyez closed her eyes, preparing herself for her first spider kiss. She had been told that spiders were great kissers. Not as good as red ants (who were renowned all over the world for having thick, pouting lips, and curly tongues) but they were right up there near the top of the pile in the snogging stakes.

She waited, and Bongo edged nearer.

Suddenly, out of the darkness, popped the worried looking face of the tailless rat, the light on top of his head flashing frantically. He unknowingly parted the romantic couple with his snout.

'Quick... quick; help me.... they've gone.... they've gone,' Duggan spurted out the words.

'Slow down Duggan,' Bongo tried to calm the irate rat, 'who's gone? What are you talking about?'

'They've gone. My uncle will kill me!'

'Who's gone?'

'The snails.' He grabbed Bongo by his neck. 'The family of French snails have gone. One minute they were taking in the sights, the next...Powwow... they disappeared in a puff of smoke.'

The rodent ran aimlessly around the body of the giant.

Greeneyez decided to speak, 'Perhaps they just went for a stroll!'

Duggan stopped dead in his tracks for the second time that night. He sauntered up to the fly and cried, 'A stroll... perhaps they have gone for a stroll.' His voice was at fever pitch. 'They are snails....not donkeys on a picnic. We were on the beach. You would have thought that perhaps I would have noticed a family of snails STROLLING their way up the sands. It would have taken them about three years to get to the pier.'

'Have you told anyone?' Bongo asked.

'About what?' Duggan had tears in his eyes.

'About the snails…. What do you think I was talking about…the price of potato peelings?'

Duggan sat down, and put his little head in his paws, and wiped away a tear. This was the end for him. His uncle would sack him for sure this time. He had been given too many warnings in the past. Especially after the episode when he had somehow misplaced that pregnant earwig who he had been taking to the hospital. How she ended up on a slave ship heading for the South Seas was still a mystery to him.

The crying from the rat got louder.

'Did you tell anyone about the dead body?' Bongo asked.

'No!…. no!.' Duggan didn't sound convincing. He would have sounded more believable if he had told them that he wasn't really a rat but a pirate called Shark-face, who was captain on a ghost ship.

The fly and spider looked at him suspiciously.

'Well, only a couple of insects.' He left a pause before slowly adding, 'And a few rats…. and some passing seagulls, three dogs and some performing flies from a travelling circus, who were very friendly. But I didn't tell them much.'

'What did you tell them exactly, Duggan?'

'Well... hmmmm. What was the question again?' The rat was looking for a way out.

'What did you tell the entire insect population about the dead body?' Bongo was getting angry. He looked at Greeneyez.

'Oh that question!... I only told them that we had found a nice juicy dead giant, with his throat cut, underneath the pier... that's all.'

Before Bongo had time to reply, off in the distance they could hear a low rumbling sound heading towards them. Neither of them said a thing at first. The noise reminded Greeneyez of the trams that wormed their way through the busy Dublin streets.

It got louder and louder. The three turned their heads and suddenly, from behind the wooden pillars that held the pier in position, they saw a carpet of insects, of every kind, racing towards them.

The posse of insects were carrying, or dragging, all kinds of objects, buckets, spades, tobacco-leaf carrier-bags, in their tiny hands, legs, or tucked behind their wings. The blanket of creepy-crawlies, on seeing the large stiff body lying lifeless in the sand, suddenly stopped in one big line

At the front an earwig held up the two hundred and fifty three toes of his left feet, before yelling, 'Ok insects of Tiger-Moth Bay... It's meal-time.'

Within five seconds flat (if you were counting in giants time or nearly ten days in insect time), the corpse, that only several hours earlier had been planning a new life in America, was awash with hungry insects, intent on picking its bones clean for a meal to share out amongst their families.

Bongo and Greeneyez' romantic moment had sadly come to an abrupt end. Bongo knew it had been great while it lasted, and he hoped that they could do it all again tomorrow. Sadly nothing in Tiger-Moth Bay was certain, and unfortunately sometimes tomorrow had a habit of not turning up.

The young lovers both jumped off the body, landing in the soft, yellow sand, just as the rest of the starving insects clambered on. They walked arm-in-leg back towards Buzztown. It was ten to ten, and Bongo realised that he needed to get Greeneyez home soon, or her mother would be worrying that he really was the infamous 'Bluebottle Eater of Dublin.'

Meanwhile, Duggan was still running around the body frantically. He kept stopping insects while they were feasting, to see if any of them had come across a family of garlic-smelling snails.

Chapter 8

'The Emperor decides on supper'

Emperor Balasz opened his set of evil red eyes and stretched out on his king-sized bed. He was surrounded, as usual, by his harem that he had brought with him to pamper him, and basically keep him warm during the trip.

The lady-spiders tried everything to get the Emperor to relax, and to put him in a good mood. But he was bored, restless, and, more worryingly, (especially for his war cabinet and anyone else in the vicinity) he was feeling old. He felt tired, and had lost that spring in his step.

Over the last few years he had tried everything to slow down the moulting process.

On expert advice he'd drank virginal maggot's blood every other day and bathed in coconut milk before he retired to bed.

Nothing seemed to work.

The coconut milk had just made his skin go crinkly, and the constant blood-drinking had turned his eyes a nasty shade of deep red.

Back in his native homeland, during his growing desperation to stop growing old, and halt the moults, he had summoned every witch-doctor spider from all the dark corners of the country.

The witch-doctor spiders turned up in grass skirts and wild, sticky-up hair, and proceeded to rub him with potions that smelt of cattle dung. Others would smother him in magical oils that only made him come out in a rash.

Still nothing worked.

Every year, at exactly the same time, during the end of the summer period, the moulting started. After each shedding of new skin, the mirror made look him look his age. Wrinkles appeared like road maps around his deep red, bloodstained eyes and his skin sagged like loose bandages around his once powerful legs.

Each year he got more irritable. As time progressed his patience grew shorter and shorter. Each year saw another couple of decapitated witch-doctor spider's heads (with the wild, sticky-up hair) decorating the wall of his room. He wasn't known for suffering fools, or fake witch-doctor spiders, with wild, sticky-up haircuts.

The Emperor had all but given up on ever finding a miracle cure, when a passing travelling trap-door spider, who was on a ship-hopping, year off, college cruise, around the big, round world thing, informed him about this wondrous city, where all the insects lived together during summertime.

Of course, this tale of insect friendship bored the Emperor to the point where he was just about to have the trap-door spider executed. But it was then that the traveller happened to mention that in this city there was a legendary belt called the 'Belt of Kings', which had magical and mystical powers.

Emperor Balasz's eyes came alive as the traveller shared with him the stories of how the 'Belt of Kings' had apparently made lost limbs grow back, and had turned old insects young again.

'How young did they become?' Balasz demanded to know, bouncing up and down like a spiderling on his first day at school.

'Young; very young. I heard of one old beetle that couldn't walk unless he had the aide of matchsticks. He touched the 'Belt' once, and next morning he woke up... as young as the dew on the morning grass.'

Balasz was ecstatic. He listened to the story over and over again. He was over the moon! He was suitably blinded by the exaggerated fable, not to question the one, or two obvious flaws in the tale.

He even believed the part about when the old beetle with the young legs had not only walked away without his sticks, but had also entered the all-Ireland river dance championships, and had won. This, of course, was a typical insect lie, because beetles weren't allowed to enter the all-Ireland river dance championships. River dancing was a purely giant people thing.

But Balasz had been waiting for ages to hear something like this, and he wasn't going to leave a little piece of trivia like that prevent him from achieving his dream of living forever. He wanted to be the first spider to moult a thousand skins, and rule the insect world until the end of time.

Emperor Balasz persuaded the reluctant traveller to tell him the exact location of this magical 'Belt'. When the directions had been checked out and confirmed by the spider responsible for 'Checking Out Strange Locations,' Balasz had the travelling trap-door spider thrown into a vat of candle oil and dumped in a rotten tree stump.

He immediately assembled his vast array of spider troops. Before dawn broke they sailed off on the banana ship to the city called Dublin, and hopefully towards the object that would change the evil, and repulsive Emperor's life forever.

Back on the banana ship he woke up on another sunny Dublin morning. He wallowed in the idea and soaked in the anticipation of what it would be like when he had his paws on the 'Belt', while being fed some ripe grapes by a female-spider.

A sharp knock on the door snapped him back to the present, and the more pressing objective of finding the damned 'Belt' before it was too late.

Ten minutes later, he stormed into the large court room, where the family of French snails were tied to a wooden spit over a small fire.

'They'd better have some more information for me… or heads will….POP!' the Emperor yelled loudly, as he slithered up to his throne.

Each member of his war cabinet automatically placed their front legs onto their heads just in case their brains went splattering all over the walls.

Behind him, Bollo, the muscular bodyguard cranked the crab claw up a notch, and smirked. He then clapped his huge pads mischievously. Everyone jumped. The 'General for Thinking Happy Thoughts' fainted.

'What's that terrible smell?' Balasz demanded, pacing around in his beetle cloak. 'It's not that ugly crab with that awful body odour again… is it? I though we had got rid of him.'

'No… it's those slugs that we picked up on the beach,' the leader of the scouting party answered back, pointing towards the dark coloured creatures going around on the spits.

'Ve is not slugs,' one of the snails protested, and spat on the floor. 'Ve is snails,'

Emperor Balasz shrugged his shoulders in confusion, wondering what the hell the creature was talking about. He ignored the cries from the snails that were being slowly roasted on the spit, and he yelled at one of them.

'Look! Shut-up, slimy thing… I don't care if you are snails, slugs, or plain old maggots, I just want you to answer my question.'

'Ve is not saying a thing... until ve has an apology off that one who called us slugs,' the snail followed his words with a long outburst in French.

Emperor Balasz turned cold. He didn't take kindly to threats, especially if that threat was from a slimy thing that smelt of garlic, and was hanging upside down. 'We'll see.' He motioned to Bollo to pile more wood on the fire.

He slumped back on his throne and waited. Eyes fixed, toes tapping. He loved to wait especially when someone was going to suffer excruciating pain.

The temperature started to rise. Flames licked at the bare behinds of the snails. After a short while, the snail who had unwittingly started the conversation, spoke up, and said pitifully, 'Monsieur.... monsieur Ok... Ok... What do you vant to know? I vill tell you everything, but just put out ze fire... please!'

Balasz walked towards him and asked again, 'Have you seen the 'Belt of Kings?'

'Mais oui! It was vondrous! No one comes to Dublin and leaves without seeing the 'Belt of Kings'. It's like going to Paris and not sampling our gourmet food, or travelling to Spain and not…..'

Balasz stopped him in his tracks. 'I don't care about going to bloody Paris or Spain,' he screamed. 'I just want to know if you have seen it.'

'Yes, it was vonderful. Magnifique! So fantastique!...' the snail said. 'It was like the time I went to….'

Emperor Balasz grabbed the sweaty snail by the face. 'Look you... if you go off on a tangent again and continue beating around the bush, I'll have Bollo, over there, beat you with one. Now where is my 'Belt of Kings?'

In the background, the 'First Lady Commander for Finding Things' feverishly took notes.

'Vill you let us go?' the snail pleaded.

'Of course; of course,' the Emperor smoothed the snails shiny, but freshly scorched skin. 'I promise you. You and your family will be my guests. Hopefully you can stay around for lunch.' The spider licked his lips.

The snail told him that the beautiful belt was in a safe place that was in the centre of town. 'It's in the vaults, opposite the palace.'

The Emperor immediately summoned his special battalion of storm trooper spiders and informed them that they would go and search the mainland within the next thirty minutes.

As Balasz began to walk out of the room to get ready to go ashore, one of the spiders asked him what he should do with the snails.

The snail who had told him all he wanted to know, smiled across at the Emperor sympathetically. The snail was fully expecting to hear the Emperor utter a sentence with the words 'Release the snails' and 'Beds for the night' in it.

But the Emperor had got what he wanted. He looked back and stared at the snails which were still on the spit. Without hesitation the evil tyrant said

'Cook those smelly, garlic-eating slugs on a steady heat for two hours and I'll have them with a nice rum and banana sauce… when I return.'

'You spider pig-dog,' the snail yelled at him.

The butt of the crab claw, swung by Bollo the bodyguard, ensured that it would be the last thing the snail would ever shout again.

Chapter 9

'Snatch and grub'

The special battalion of storm trooper spiders, led personally by the Emperor, landed on dry land. The day was turning dramatically to dusk, allowing shadows to venture out to play.

Insect passport control that patrolled the bay ensuring that no illegal insect immigrants landed on the shores, sadly didn't stand a chance as the killer-spiders crushed everything in their path.

The battalion moved swiftly through the darkness in perfect formation. They didn't speak. They had been trained not to. Leg signals and the rolling of eyes mapped out their route. A trail of destruction was left in their wake, as Emperor Balasz, who was held high above them, pushed onwards with his driving, and frighteningly sadistic ambition.

An unfortunate down-and-out woodlouse, whose only crime was to be a little down on his luck and sleeping off a hangover, between a wall and the pavement, was asked directions, and then trampled to death by the rolling black army.

Surveillance had pin-pointed the location of the vault, which housed the prized 'Belt'. When they eventually reached their destination, the spider marauders silently surrounded the building. On the signal from Bollo, the bodyguard, they proceeded to smash down the heavy doors.

The place was deadly quiet, except for the sound of snoring coming up from a small, wooden desk at the back of the room.

The soldier-spiders automatically fanned out in formation, working tirelessly, searching, and destroying anything that didn't resemble some kind of belt-thing.

The silence was broken when one spider whistled. Bollo marched towards the soldier who stood to attention by the large oil lamp in the centre of the room.

'Do you think this is it?' the soldier-spider asked his superior.

Before the bodyguard had chance to investigate and comment on his assessment of the contents behind the glass part of the old lamp, Emperor Balasz slithered triumphantly into the room.

'Yes it is!' his voice rose high like smoke from a chimney. 'That is my 'Belt of Kings'.' He scuttled up to the old oil lamp in a flash, smashing the protective glass with a sharp object. He grabbed the 'Belt', lifting it up high above his head, parading it in ultimate triumph.

The other spiders' weren't sure if they should clap, bow, or just stand to attention.

They looked for guidance from Bollo, the bodyguard. He obediently dropped to four knees, lowering his eyes to the ground. The rest copied the bodyguard's actions.

Suddenly, from out behind the desk, Uncle Paddy 'O' Dacey jumped up, still suffering from the mother of all hangovers, and seeing everything in double.

'What round is it? Am I cut?'

Everyone in the room turned and stared in disbelief at the large daddy long-legs spider, who was now shadow boxing with himself.

Uncle Paddy stopped jigging about, and dipped his head in a bowl of rainwater. He could now see more clearly, but still saw two of everything. He motioned towards the Emperor, who hadn't even acknowledged the disturbance that the daddy long-legs spider was causing. He was more interested in the sheer beauty of the item in his possession, and its everlasting power that it would provide.

'Hey, what are you twins doing with my 'Belts'?' Uncle Paddy shouted at the skinny black spider holding up the treasure.

'It's mine now. This 'Belt' is coming with me.' Balasz replied coldly.

Uncle Paddy was very impressed how the two spiders, which incidentally looked exactly the same, had also spoken, and moved, at exactly the same time.

Emperor Balasz clicked his little finger-things on his legs and three obedient soldier-spiders rushed towards the swaying Irish spider. Although Uncle Paddy was getting on a bit in years and many drinking sessions had pickled his mind, he could still slug it out with the best of them.

His first hay-maker punch sent the leading on-coming insect crashing into the wall, dislodging a portrait of last year's mayor, which then fell on his head. The brawl had started to clear Uncle Paddy's mind enough to allow him to start to focus normally.

Next, he followed up with a left, right combination that stunned the second soldier, and a vicious upper-cut despatched the last one to dreamland.

'So... it's a rumble, you'll be a-wanting!' he calmly said, rolling up his shirt sleeves.

Three more soldiers joined in the scrap, and met with more, or less, the same fate. Uncle Paddy's famous, and powerful right leg, was now causing maximum damage and banana spider destruction.

Unconscious soldier-spiders lay motionless all around.

Just as Uncle Paddy was beginning to fully enjoy himself, the crowd of spiders parted and Bollo, the big muscled bodyguard, strolled through the crowd.

'The bigger they are, the harder they fall,' Uncle Paddy muttered to himself, as he took up his Queensbury rules boxing stance.

Although Bollo was very large, and looked like the side of a shoe box, and could usually beat most spiders just by sneering at them, he was an extremely crafty fighter, one who prided himself on fighting dirty. He didn't really need to because of his size, but he found that it added something to the victory, and ensured he kept his rugged good looks.

Bollo threw the sand into the eyes of the Irish daddy long-legs, momentarily blinding the spider long enough for the crab's claw to connect squarely with the side of his head, knocking Uncle Paddy out cold.

'Who's the daddy long-legs now, then?' hissed Bollo, throwing his legs into the air.

The rest of the soldier spiders' cheered wildly. 'Bollo, Bollo, Bollo.'

'Enough,' screamed Emperor Balasz.

'That was one mean right leg on that brute,' Emperor Balasz said, before turning to his 'Commander for Ripping Parts off the Body of Other Insects and Displaying Them on the Emperor's Wall,' and informed him that he wanted the limb on the wall of his trophy cabinet.

As the Emperor proudly paraded out of the vault still holding the 'Belt of Kings' high above his head, at least twenty-three storm trooper spiders, on instructions from the 'Commander for Ripping Parts off the Body of Other Insects to Displaying Them on the Emperor's Wall,' pulled and tugged for fifteen minutes on the right leg of Uncle Paddy.

Eventually, the leg, ripped and torn, then popped out of the socket of the unconscious spider.

Uncle Paddy lay there dreaming that someone was pulling his leg, but for some strange reason he was finding it hard to get the joke.

The remaining soldiers proceeded to leave and the vault was left deserted.

Chapter 10

'Something's wrong'

As the ship carrying the cargo of bananas was unloaded onto the unsuspecting dockside, thousands upon thousands of Balasz's troops spilled onto the cobbled pavement. Even the giant people stepped aside as the black mass disappeared under pier 14.

Emperor Balasz had not only stolen the 'Belt of Kings', he had also acquisitioned the Mayor's 'fishing boat turned upside down' palace. Once inside, he had instructed his bodyguards to hang up Terry (the bilingual woodlouse mayor) from his neck in the newly converted war room.

Although Terry the woodlouse had been dangling by the throat for a while, he was far from dead. What the banana spiders hadn't accounted for was the hard shell around the woodlouse's neck that prevented the rope from applying enough pressure to strangle the poor creepy-crawly.

But due to all the hanging around with no food or drink, and the fact that most of his blood had gathered down amongst his many toes, Terry was extremely weak and had started to hallucinate. He believed he was now a Spanish matador called Enrico, who was the youngest brother in a family of nine that lived on a tomato farm.

This observation was made even weirder, because Terry had never seen or heard of a tomato before, or even a bull.

By mid-day the banana spider army had been instructed to occupy the streets, rounding up hordes of insects of every colour and creed. Tea-chests were emptied of their contents onto the warehouse floor and made ready for a new and more sinister role as make-shift concentration camps.

Bongo was unaware of events that were unfolding down in the centre of Tiger-Moth Bay. He hadn't been able to sleep that morning. He had gone for a long scuffle as the big, shiny, yellow round thing poked its face over the horizon. The young spider was walking on air since his first date with the fly.

He found himself all alone, sitting in an empty pipe, little legs dangling over the side. He was all too aware that sadly the romance between him and Greeneyez couldn't last. The sunnytime would soon disappear and that would mean that his new girl-fly of today, could possibly end up as a Sunday roast for his family tomorrow. A harrowing, but sobering, thought.

He knew that it wasn't fair, but sadly lots of the activities that took place daily on the wild side of the docks weren't designed to be fair. It was all about survival.

He had an idea that perhaps they could elope, like his cousin Cecil, who had apparently fallen in love and run away with a centipede, half his age. But he remembered how the runaway lovers had been caught and brought back. His cousin Cecil had been sent away to a special school by the insects with the white wings, and no one set eyes on poor Cecil again.

Bongo also realised that a spider and a fly wouldn't be accepted wherever they ended up. There were no mixed insect marriages to speak of, but that was not to say that mixed relationships didn't take place once in a while.

The spider had seen first hand the resulting offspring of a brief drunken encounter between a female butterfly and a red blooded male ant. It hadn't been a pretty sight. The children were treated as freaks and the entire abnormal family were eventually banished and made to go and live in 'Insect Forgotten City.'

Bongo had sat for hours overlooking Tiger-Moth Bay contemplating the future, until he suddenly felt distinctly hungry, and he headed home. He swirled and whirled his way back through the old familiar streets.

The teenage insect couldn't put his leg on it, but he felt that something terrible had happened. Something was wrong. He hurriedly scampered through the alleyway, past the Chinese linen basket and into the cul-de-sac, where his boot home stood.

The place was strangely deserted. An eerie silence followed his every footstep. There was no smell of breakfast that usually tickled his nostrils at about this point in the journey. There was nothing to greet him, in fact no sounds or smell at all.

As he got closer to his house boot, he noticed that the door had been kicked off its hinges.

The young spider frantically rushed into the front room. His heart was beating fast. The room had been ransacked and turned upside down. Pictures were off the wall, furniture was destroyed, cupboards overturned. Bongo's drum kit was smashed to smithereens. It took him several minutes for the shock to sink in.

A low moaning sound from above had the young spider bounding upstairs in a flash. Bongo let out a cry on seeing his older brother covered in some strange foreign web-spit. A darning needle pierced his side, impaling him to the leather floor.

'What's happened? Who's done this? Where's Mam and the rest?' The speed of the questions entangled themselves in a knot as they raced out of Bongo's mouth.

'Black spiders…. hundreds of them. They were speaking in a language that I have never heard before.' His brother's voice was weak.

Gooey blood which trickled from his brother's wound made the floor sticky and red.

His brother continued, 'They overpowered me….. They've taken Mam, the kids and the rest of the neighbours.'

Bongo attempted to pull out the pin.

His brother winced. 'It's too late Bongo…. You're the father of the family now. It's up to you to get them back…. It's up to you to save Dublin. It's up to you…' Bongo's brother closed his eyes. His last breath escaped from his chest and floated towards the heavens.

Tears the size of raindrops, rolled down the young spider's face, as he buried his brother in the backyard. His head was spinning for the second time that day. He didn't know which way to turn. He needed to talk to someone.

It was then that he remembered Greeneyez.

He started to sprint through the deserted streets as fast as his eight legs could carry him. The image of her beautiful face spurred him on faster. A short while later he reached the archway to Buzztown, only it was different now. The neon sign was on the ground, smashed into a million pieces.

Bongo didn't hesitate about entering this time around as he furiously raced in Buzztown. The streets were exactly the same as he had found in Spiderville, except there were lots of male flies lying dead amongst the rotten vegetables. The place smelt worse than ever, added to by the houses burning and scorched blue bottle wings.

He finally reached number 76, Legless Spider Lane. It was empty. He knew it would be, but he lived in hope. He didn't know if it being deserted was a good or bad sign. But he knew it was a sign of some kind.

He spent the next two hours wandering through the other streets that only a day earlier had been bustling with insect life. There was no sound. No life…. nothing.

Suddenly, a splintering noise rose up from behind him. Bongo ducked and dived behind some debris. He waited, trembling in fear. When he saw who it was he couldn't help but smile. Bongo had never thought he would ever see the day when he would hear himself saying the following words with such meaning. They escaped from out of his mouth with pleasure. 'Hello Duggan, I'm so glad to see you.'

He watched with joy as the tailless rodent was having enormous difficulty trying to squeeze his backside out of a broken drainpipe.

Chapter 11

'Finding Uncle Paddy'

'What's happening Duggan? What the hell is going on?' Bongo asked tearfully, as the reality of laying his brother to rest earlier that morning suddenly descended over him like a black cloud.

'I think my African princess wants to finish with me! She's acting awfully strange... she never returns my calls….and her father…'

'Not with your love life….you idiot. Or with that supposedly made-up chief with the stupid zebra bone in his made-up snout,' Bongo yelled, throwing his cap at the rat. 'What's happening in the docks? Where have all the insects gone?

Duggan looked shocked. He shook his head from side to side, then back and forth, and finally up and down.

'I hadn't noticed… honest Bongo…. I really hadn't noticed. But I'm not paid to take notice of things… I'm paid to transport you lot around the Bay.'

Bongo started to cry, 'My family's gone, my brother's dead, Greeneyez is missing.'

'What did you say? Your brother's what?' The rat's ears pricked up sharply.

'My brother's dead! Someone murdered him!'

'Are you sure?' Duggan become nervous. It showed in his nonsensical questions.

Bongo voice had a hint of anger, 'Yes of course I'm sure! I buried him two hours ago. Someone… or something had beaten him to death.'

'Who done it?.... was it giants?…. Was it those nasty tomcats?….or maybe those beetles? Quick lets go and seek revenge.'

'Before he died he said something about black spiders…. Evil black banana spiders talking in a foreign language,' Bongo replied, before slumping down on a flat stone. 'He told me it was up to me to save Dublin city.'

'Oh no… not banana spiders. Ain't they those big hairy ones?' Duggan didn't want Bongo to actually say 'yes.'

Bongo had to think fast. It was time for him to turn all his thoughts into working out a plan. That's what his brother would have done. But thinking didn't come naturally to Bongo at the best of times; never mind being accountable for devising a plan. His mind was awash with many thoughts, but he needed to link them together so maybe they could form some sort of pattern.

Duggan sat opposite, picking dry leaves out of his toes.

'I'm sure I've stood on something sharp.' The rat declared inspecting his feet. 'Am I cut?' he asked Bongo.

The last three words the rodent muttered lit a light bulb in the young spider's mind, which was fully responsible for illuminating the first step of some sort of crude plan of what they should do next.

'My Uncle Paddy.'

'Where?' replied Duggan, looking around.

'No he's not here! But my Uncle Paddy will know what to do and what's going on,' he said before quickly adding, 'and he'll track the murderers down and rip them to shreds,'

Bongo just hoped that he wouldn't find Uncle Paddy drunk and asleep behind a desk. 'Quick Duggan…. to the vaults.'

They arrived in treble quick speed. This was mainly due to the fact that, other than the giant people's big boots that stomped about completely unaware of the struggles down below in Tiger-Moth Bay, there had been no other creepy-crawlies to hinder their journey.

Bongo shrieked to himself on seeing the big door that once stood so grand in the entrance to the secret vaults lying helpless on the floor. He shrieked even louder when he saw the shattered remains of the glass oil lamp case which had housed the precious 'Belt of Kings'. The magical belt of Dublin town was gone.

'This is bad, real bad,' he thought to himself.

Bongo let out an enormous yell which he followed closely with an extra large shriek, when Duggan accidentally slid on a pool of blood that covered the floor.

'My Uncle Paddy.... what's happened to my Uncle Paddy?' Bongo ran over to the desk that was laying helpless on its side.

No one was behind it.

The trail of blood snaked its way out of the vault, across the narrow street and headed towards the centre of town. Bongo jumped on the rat's back and instructed him to follow the sticky red substance.

They slowly trotted west for about hundred metres. Although they still hadn't seen any other living insects, sadly they had come across many dead or dying along the way. They treaded with care through the silent streets. The entire place had been covered in some unusual silk thread.

'I think we've come far enough.' Duggan explained. On his face was the expression of someone who had found themself on the wrong side of the crack in a pavement in a very bad neighbourhood.

'But the trail continues up that alleyway towards that big building with the pointy top,' Bongo snapped.

'Do you know where it leads to?' Duggan stopped walking. A certain dread crept into his voice, as he turned around to face his passenger. Bongo innocently shrugged his little shoulders.

'Beats me.'

'Down there is the giant people's chapel.' He shuddered. 'That's where all the weird insects hang out. That's where 'Insect Forgotten City' is.' A flicker of fear ran in front of the rat's eyes.

Bongo silently repeated the words with which Duggan had just enlightened him. The spider had heard some frightening stories about 'Insect Forgotten City'. He knew that Duggan's taxi firm never took anybody beyond this point.

But Bongo had come this far. His Uncle was hurt; he wasn't going to turn back now.

'Come on Duggan….Are you a rat or a mouse? My uncle's in some sort of trouble. The city's in trouble. We have got to find him. He's our only hope.'

Duggan thought that the 'mouse' wisecrack was well below the belt. He decided to continued, but his steps became shorter and shorter, as the alleyway became darker and darker. They came to a dead end. Facing them was a big wall made from stone. In the wall there was a small, dark passageway that led into the cemetery. It was much too small for the rat to fit through. The spider could tell that Duggan was secretly pleased. From where he was sitting he could feel the fear racing through the rat.

He realised that Duggan would never squeeze through the chink in the mortar that undoubtedly led to the mysterious place where apparently 'Insects went to either forget or be forgotten.

Bongo told Duggan to wait for him. This frightened the rat even more and he hid behind a rubbish bin, switching off the light on his head.

Bongo took a deep breath and climbed into the hole. He could already feel his chest tightening, but this was not the time or place to start a bout of coughing. He picked up a short but substantial piece of timber and followed the fresh trail of blood into the dark hole in the wall.

Down and down he went. The passageway soon turned into a tunnel that was pitch black. It was so dark, it was actually lighter when Bongo closed his eyes. This is what the young spider did, until he fell out of the tunnel, landing heavily on a pile of earth.

He got up and brushed himself down. He knew he was being watched. Spiders have a built in radar that can sense any kind of danger. He continued cautiously to follow the droplets of blood.

'Hey you…. young one,' a voice from a gloomy doorway asked, 'would you like a nice maggot….freshly caught this morning.'

Bongo quickened his pace and walked on, not daring to glance back.

Just past a discarded gin bottle, he bumped head-first into an ageing old spider with only one leg. In front of him, he had words written on a piece of card in big bold lettering:

'Veteran of the giant Grasshopper crusade 1935… Wife and 314 children to support… please give generously.'

The war veteran looked Bongo up and down. 'Long way from home…boy. Running from the truth, family troubles, or searching for the real you? Well whatever it is…you're in the right place.'

Bongo's throat was dry, but he managed to whisper, 'Sorry sir…it's none of what you just mentioned. I'm just looking for someone.'

'Oh…' the one-legged insect commented. 'Yeah, I see. We get a lot of young healthy creatures like you, crawling in, looking to satisfy their cravings. They are over there, if you must know.' If the veteran had any spare legs he would have pointed out the directions.

'Who are over there?' Bongo said innocently.

'The ladybirds of the night. You know… the good time girls. They all hang out over by the large gravestone with the stone demons on top. But let me give you some friendly advice, though.'

Bongo tried to interrupt quickly, but was too slow.

'Make sure it's a ladybird that you are getting. Know what I mean. Some of those ladyboys… I swear you can't tell the difference…. Well not until you get past the spots anyway.' He chuckled to himself.

Horror and disgust was cemented onto Bongo's face. 'No… no. I'm searching for my uncle. You must have seen him passing recently.' Bongo pointed towards the trail of blood that covered the ground. 'He's used to be the insect boxing champion of the entire world.'

The veteran laughed. It was a laugh that Bongo didn't appreciate. It sounded false and mickey-taking.

Angrily Bongo added, 'He was the boxing champion! He beat a grasshopper for the title. He stopped him in the eighth round with an upper cut.'

'Look kid... I see them all pass this way. Ex-boxing champions... movie stars, the rich and famous...you name them.... They have all been to 'Insect Forgotten City.'

Bongo pointed to the blood on the grass. 'But you must have seen him... he was injured.'

'I don't see anything that I'm not supposed to,' the insect's reply was sharp and precise.

The veteran could see the disappointment on Bongo's face. He felt a little pity for the good looking teenager. 'Look... If he did pass, and I'm not saying that he did, I bet he would have headed for Sam's place.... It's about ten graves over, way down in the crypt.'

He thanked the veteran and wished that he had some coins to place in his tin. But he didn't. He walked gingerly away.

Bongo had heard about Sam's Place.

He had once overheard his late father whispering a story about the secrets of the public house to his Uncle Paddy, while the adult spiders drank the giant people's potent brew in the kitchen.

'You won't believe what happened next,' he had heard his father giggling. 'There, on stage, was this insect.... called Sticky Licky.' His voice lowered another notch, 'Should have seen what she did with a grain of rice?'

'She's one dirty stick-insect,' his Uncle Paddy had quickly replied.

Bongo recalled the adult spiders' laughter filling every inch of the old boot.

Back in the eerie surroundings of the cemetery, Bongo thankfully reached the outside of Sam's Place.

The entrance was a damaged urn, tipped onto its side. Above the door was a plain black sign that announced that this was the best place in town…bar none.

'Best place for what?' Bongo thought to himself.

On the door someone had written in the dust. 'You don't need to be ugly, fat or even a woodlouse to drink here…. but it does help!'

Before the teenager entered, he took a long intake of air, and then he slowly followed the blood trail into the blackness of Sam's Place.

The crypt had individual tables laid out around the perimeter of the dark room. The lighting was purposely designed to leave a lot to the imagination. A small stage was tucked away near the back.

Bongo could smell insect women's perfume, mixed with the strong aroma of rice grains. He rightly thought that he must have just missed Sticky Licky doing her nightly spot.

Running down the left hand side of the crypt was an enormous bar, and occupying a space behind it was a caterpillar, with a rather large head, who Bongo assumed was Sam the owner.

Bongo rotated his eyes in a clockwise motion so that he could see all the corners of the place at once, a trick his brother had taught him. He did notice some strange things.

Up by the toilets he spotted a blind moth drinking alone; the moth appeared to have been crying heavily. At the next table were two brightly coloured green ants, heads slumped in greener drinks. In the cubicle opposite sat a fly in a pool of his own saliva. It took Bongo a while to work out that the poor insect didn't have any wings.

He pulled up a bar-stool and waited to speak to the caterpillar with the large head.

Sitting on the barstool next to him was a creepy-crawly that first appeared to Bongo to be just your average run of the mill earwig. But on closer inspection he discovered, to his horror, that it was in fact a slow worm in earwigs clothing.

He felt like running away or going to the bathroom to throw up. He had been warned that cross-dressing insects existed but this was the first time he had actually seen one in the flesh. 'Or in someone else's flesh' He giggled out loud at his own private little joke.

'Hey…. what's so funny?' the slow-worm (come earwig) asked, obviously a little bit touchy in the 'insects laughing to themselves at the bar' department.

'Nothing!' Bongo's eyes refused to make contact with the weirdo.

'Fancy a shot?' the slow-worm asked, offering out a hand in friendship.

Bongo shook his hand and immediately noticed the odd creature had orange painted toe-nails.

'No thank you, mister….hmmm' Bongo struggled with what to call the orange thing.

'Hey, kid. There's no need for you to call me mister. This is an informal bar. Just call me Eric. It's Eric the earwig.'

Bongo would have let out a deep laugh, if he hadn't been so nervous. He bit his tongue hard.

'What are you doing here anyway kid? You're a long way from home,' Eric said, while straightening his orange tights.

'I'm waiting to ask Sam something,' the young spider replied, pointing towards the caterpillar with the large head, who was up the other end of the bar entertaining some punters by balancing a rusty spoon on his nose.

Bongo continued in a pleading voice, 'I need to know if he's seen my Uncle Paddy come in here.'

Now it was Eric, the pretend earwig's turn for a little chuckle to himself. 'That's not Sam; Sam's dead.' He answered gleefully.

Bongo stiffened up on the barstool.

The slow-worm carefully applied some orange lipstick before adding, 'Sam was killed, or to be more precise, murdered, last winter in some three-way gay insect love triangle. That's Sam's ex-partner, Big Taff. And I'm afraid he won't tell you anything.'

Bongo was beginning to realise just how sick and twisted this place really was. He had only just got here, but he had already witnessed day-glo green ants, one-legged war veterans, ladybirds on the game, slow-worms who insisted that they were earwigs, and heard stories of bizarre bar-creatures getting murdered in gay love-triangle affairs… whatever next?

He was both afraid and intrigued.

He probed a little deeper about Big Taff. 'But why won't he tell me anything? Is he upset because of Sam?'

Another loud laugh rose up from the cross-dresser on the next bar stool.

'You are funny,' Eric gestured to Bongo. 'You do make me laugh.'

'I'm funny,' Bongo thought to himself. 'I make you laugh… I'm not the one sitting all alone in this desperate place, dressed in an orange jump-suit and nail varnish.'

Eric tried to untangle the confusion that was surrounding their conversation. 'No…..Big Taff wasn't Sam's lover.'

'You said he was his partner.' Bongo was now more confused than ever.

'He was his business partner, not his partner, partner!' Eric looked at the young spider as if he was a freak. 'No! Big Taff's as straight as it gets. You should see his misses; what a beauty?'

Bongo stared into Eric's face to try and get him back on track. 'OK, but why won't he tell me if he's seen my Uncle Paddy?'

'Because he's Welsh, if you must know and.... his tongue's been cut out.'

'Why was his tongue cut out?' he asked the most obvious question first.

Eric edged in a little closer to Bongo and whispered, 'Cheating at cards. That's not a wise thing to do when you play five card poker with the Sonkie brothers. Those are two evil and nasty butterflies.'

Bongo was fully and utterly enthralled in the conversation. He could imagine how being tongue-less may stop the caterpillar with the large head communicating with him, but he wasn't at all sure why being Welsh would stop him telling him about the possible whereabouts of his Uncle. So he asked the slow-worm again.

Eric shook his head and muttered, 'Because he can't understand a word of English... that's why. Whatever you ask him, he just pours you a pint and does a bad impression of an Irish jig. Watch this.' Eric waved to the Caterpillar who came over with the spoon still balancing on his nose.

'Hey! Big Taffy...give us two mugs of your finest malt whiskey and two cigars.'

'Mmmrrggg mrrrgggggggg,' the tongue-less bar-insect muttered, before going off and pouring the earwig a cold beer, then standing on the bar and proceeding to throw his arms and legs about wildly.

Every creature in the room clapped, except for the two green ants, who were still sleeping in their drinks.

'Told you so.' The slow-worm said. 'Not just mad. He's mad, dumb, and Welsh; a lethal combination.'

'Well can you help me then?' Bongo was close to tears again. 'Have you seen my Uncle Paddy. I think he's left that trail of blood over there.' He indicated to a red spot on the sawdust.

'Yeah... why didn't you ask me in the first place? He's over there,' Eric pointed to a dark cubicle over by the emergency exit.

Bongo thanked the cross-dressing slow-worm and rushed over to the corner of the room.

He found his uncle, head slumped in a tobacco leaf of dark liquid, a homemade, blood-stained bandage over his legs.

'Uncle Paddy... its Bongo. What's happened? Where's the 'Belt of Kings' gone?'

At first the daddy long-legs didn't answer.

Bongo pulled back the red bandage and noticed the injury to the street fighter.

'Where's your bashing leg gone, Uncle Paddy?' Bongo searched under the table for any signs of it, unaware of how stupid he must have appeared.

'They've gone. They've both gone.' Uncle Paddy looked up from the table. His eyes were distant. 'The 'Belt' has been stolen by some slimy black ball called Bal-hash, or something like that.'

'But what about your leg, Uncle?'

'His soldier troops pulled my slugging leg off for fun. I'll never be champion of the world again.'

He took another long swig of the rum, before slamming his head down hard onto the table. The two drunken green ants woke up and started dancing with one another.

Bongo knew that Uncle Paddy wouldn't be champion of the world ever again, even if he did have his best slugging arm available. He was no spring chicken. He was getting on for at least twelve spider years. On top of that, he had lost his last four professional fights and had spent the last three years immersed in the demon drink.

But Bongo appreciated that perhaps this was not the time or place to mention Uncle Paddy's apparent slide down the ladder of respectability. Bongo was well aware that most insects who frequented this bar had long since skidded down that ladder, probably landing in a large wet and dirty puddle of hopelessness and despair. He needed another approach.

'Uncle Paddy, I've seen you knock them out without using the slugger.' He tried some reverse psychology.

Uncle Paddy raised his head up ever so slightly.

Bongo quickly added, 'You don't need that old slugging leg. You're a warrior! A beast! You're my Uncle Paddy, the best fighter Dublin's ever had.'

Uncle Paddy jumped up feeling a lot better. Unfortunately for the blind moth that had been crying earlier, the old street fighter decided to see if his nephew was right. He launched the blind moth across the room with a punch from his left. The poor insect landed on top of the fly with no wings.

Everyone in the bar cheered.

Bongo reacted immediately. 'Quick Uncle Paddy, we need to sober you up…. You may never be champion of the world again… but you can help save all the insects of Dublin.'

They left Sam's Place, saying goodbye to Eric and the tongue-less Welsh caterpillar with the large head, who was still jigging on the bar, but was now attempting to sing a song as well.

As Bongo walked through the doors, he'd found it extremely odd that although no one could understand a word that the tongue-less Welsh caterpillar with the large head was actually singing, they all joined in on the chorus.

Chapter 12

'Cocooned'

Several days before, Greeneyez had been soundly asleep in her pretty pink honeycomb bed, dreaming about Bongo and the dead giant, when the banana soldier-spiders arrived at her front door.

By the time she realised that something bad was happening, she and her family had been roughly man-handled (or killer spider-handled) out of their warm home and into the busy street, she could smell burning and hear lots of crying.

Her big round green eyes could see lots of things going on but she couldn't take in all of the horrific events that were unfolding in front of her.

There were houses on fire, shop windows were smashed and hundreds of black spiders were pushing and whipping the peaceful residents until they got into long lines.

She saw her own father being forcibly dragged across the street. He was trying hard to resist, so that he could protect his family. He was smacked hard in the mouth with the butt of a pine cone, by a large, brutish creature. He dropped like a stone to the ground.

Greeneyez didn't realise at the time, but that would be the last time she actually saw her old man again.

The hysterical flies were bundled together and forced into separate lines. All the woman and children were pushed to the left and the men-flies to the right.

On instruction from the spider who had hit Greeneyez' father in the mouth, the insect prisoners were all marched out of Buzztown towards the docks.

During the harsh journey, the black spiders screamed and yelled uncontrollably at the prisoners in a language that she couldn't understand. But she appreciated from the aggression in the tone of their voices that it wasn't pleasant. She recognised the hatred etched on her captor's faces, which indicated to her that they were not just taking them on a surprise school trip to pick flowers.

Some of the older flies who couldn't keep up with the demanding pace, were beaten viciously as they fell. Their screams pierced the air. Anyone who attempted to help them was also savagely dealt with by the soldiers.

Flies in both lines, were crying.

The procession snaked its way to the end of the street and over the iron bridge. Greeneyez spied another line of insects by the spot where the old rusty anchor lay horizontal on the cobblestones; their heads were slumped towards the ground, as they shuffled slowly their way.

The group turned out to be a large group of female woodlice, and, by their dishevelled appearance, Greeneyez could tell that they had received the same type of treatment as she and her family had suffered.

After a long, arduous march, they were finally imprisoned in a large tea-chest in an old abandoned warehouse on the Southside of the docks. The wooden crates were cold, dark, damp and smelt of coffee. The cramped space was filled with the constant sobbing of the inmates. Greeneyez crawled on her belly through the mass of bodies. She finally found her mother and six of her little sisters.

They hugged each other with joy, and then wept themselves to sleep.

The following morning, as the big, yellow, shiny thing spat rays of sunlight through the slates of the tea-chests, they were all forced out onto the pavement in front of the warehouse buildings. Greeneyez looked around her, hoping to see a friendly face.

She noticed everyone from the dockside seemed to be here. All the different species, male and female, young and old, were lined up.

She wondered where Bongo was. Her large eyes searched up and down the line of spiders, but the youngster was not amongst them. She felt a sharp pain inside as she imagined Bongo lying injured on a pavement somewhere. She used some positive thinking and kept telling herself that he was still alive.

She tried to see over the other fly heads. She was suddenly knocked over by a strong jet of water. The entire line of insects were all hosed down with freezing cold salt water and made to stand perfectly still until dry.

They were then issued with a number and, worst of all, they were cocooned in a fine silk thread and hung back up in the dark tea-chest.

There Greeneyez hung, unable to communicate with anyone else. Luckily her mother hung opposite. She couldn't see where her younger sisters were.

'Be brave,' her mother mouthed to her and blew her a kiss.

Greeneyez closed her eyes for a long time.

Each morning the door of the tea-chest was opened, and sunlight spilled into the darkness, playing tricks with the flies' eyes. Every morning the grinning black spiders would come amongst them.

She could hear them shuffling and scuffling, laughing and joking. She could see them staring and leaching. It frightened them all.

Each time they came, they would take down a handful of cocooned flies and drag them through the door and into the dazzling, warm sunlight.

As evening come and the light slowly disappeared, Greeneyez knew that those flies which had been selected earlier by the guards, wouldn't be coming back. Every day was the same.

Each morning, Greeneyez would close her lovely eyes and hold her breath, as the evil guards randomly picked their victims from the hordes of helpless hanging insects.

One morning, as the door closed behind the evil creatures, she was again thankful that she hadn't been chosen yet again. She looked across to the spot where her mother had been hanging. The spot was empty.

She cried a thousand tears all day.

Anthony Bunko

Chapter 13

'The Rat Trap'

Bongo and his Uncle Paddy left Sam's Place and found a petrified Duggan still shaking like a leaf while hiding behind the rubbish bin.

Before they all set off back towards Tiger-Moth Bay, there were a couple of things to sort out. One of the most important things was to bandage the damaged leg socket of the old street-fighting spider.

Duggan, who had attended first-aid training while working for the taxi company, volunteered to complete the operation. The rat's attempt to manufacture a sling was crude to say the least. It was uneven, and flapped about a bit around the edges, but, all in all, it did the job of patching up the old warrior.

Bongo and Uncle Paddy rode high up on the rat's back and the three lone survivors scurried through the deserted insect streets.

They were mesmerised by the silence and loneliness that greeted them wherever they went.

The only noise was the rustling of paper that blew about on the warm wind. It was eerie. It was the same desolate scene, whatever part of insect quarters they happened to ventured into.

Buzztown, Centipede Crescent, Earwig Road, Ant Alleyway, Woodlice Way, Beetle City, and Spiderville; all had been flushed clean of their occupants to be replaced by an intricate system of the finest silk webbing. It had been left by the banana spiders to act as a booby-trap to catch anyone that hadn't been rounded up and put into the tea-chests.

Duggan trod carefully, looking for any signs of life, or a signal to indicate that all was not lost.

'Where do you think they have taken them all?' Bongo asked aloud, as much to himself as to the other two.

'I've heard there's been a lot of activity down by the old battle steamer in the abandoned warehouse,' Duggan informed them both.

The rat swerved sharply to miss the full force of a well directed boot that was attached to the long legs of a drunken giant.

'But why? What do they want to do with thousands of insects?' Bongo shook his head.

Up in the sky, the big, shiny, yellow thing smiled down its warmth. It dried their throats and burnt into their skin. The heat bounced up off the dry pavements in waves. The city was humid.

Duggan had decided to share only half of what he had heard of what was going on in the abandoned warehouse. He had also been informed of the nasty rumours of why the banana spiders had assembled the insects in the tea-chests. He didn't want to panic Bongo, but he didn't know if it was the right time to part with the information. Probably for the first time in his life the talkative rodent kept quiet.

'Well, whatever they are plotting… it can't be good,' muttered Uncle Paddy, wincing as he touched the blood-stained bandage. 'I've seen some evil in my life, but never so much evil as in the eyes of that Emperor.' The daddy long-legs spat on the floor and cursed to himself.

'Look….I've got something else to tell you,' Duggan stuttered, the temptation killing him. It had taken him all of twenty seconds to spurt out the secret that was burning a hole in deep inside him.

He relayed to them what he knew. 'I've been told that the Emperor Bal-hash geezer proclaims that he is the true ruler of the insect world. He has his slimy legs on our belt and he believes that he will live forever.'

'I'll 'true ruler of the world' him when I get my legs on him,' Uncle Paddy said madly.

Duggan continued, 'I've also heard, but I don't know if there's any truth in it, that he intends to ship several tea-chests back to his homeland.'

'Well perhaps he likes tea,' Uncle Paddy was quick to reply, very obviously missing the hidden message in the rat's explanation.

'You don't understand.' Duggan stopped him in his tracks, 'the tea-chests are not full of tea.'

'He's not trying to smuggle all our rum out… is he?' Uncle Paddy's face was a picture.

'No…. not tea and not the rum. The tea-chests are full of…' The rat kicked the ground and added sheepishly, '… insects!'

Bongo didn't know if this was a tale that the rat had expanded to make himself appear more important, but he needed to find out more. 'But why Duggan? Why ship out tea-chests full of insects?' he beckoned.

'Food… food for the journey. Supposedly the Emperor was sick of living on bananas and coconut milk. He's already started to sample some of the woodlice. Apparently he has them roasted with some nutmeg and seasoning before he retires to bed.'

'But why?' Bongo could feel his heart in his mouth.

'Have you ever eaten woodlice?' Duggan contorted his face. 'They're as tough as that old boot you live in. You definitely need some nutmeg and seasoning with them.'

'And why do you think he's started with the woodlice first?' Uncle Paddy joined in the chat. 'If I was the Emperor I would have definitely started with the flies….they are more succulent.'

'Me too,' Duggan replied. 'Perhaps he's keeping them for the long journey back home….you know as a special treat.'

Bongo couldn't believe what he was listening to. He threw his cap to the floor and launched into a verbal assault on the both of them. 'Perhaps he started eating the woodlice because they start with the letter 'W'. Who knows?' he shrieked. 'Or perhaps he once had a nasty woodlice school teacher... how can you tell what goes on in the mind of a mad dictator spider?' He thought he would snap.

Bongo's mind was already upset enough just thinking of his mother and family getting transported away. Never mind the added complication of his first real girl-fly, ending up as a fly-in-a-bap sandwich for a mad dictator.

The other two realised that it was time to shut up. The following pause was distinctively awkward as they considered the plight of their love ones.

'Sorry Bongo, we didn't think,' Uncle Paddy offered his apologies.

They travelled on in silence through the deserted streets.

They eventually arrived at Canal Lane, which was the spot where the seven different streets of the seven insects' families merged into one. It led to Tiger-Moth Bay. All roads led to Tiger-Moth Bay.

Just when they had given up hope of seeing any form of insect life again, they stumbled across a black ant, firmly ensnared in the web booby-trap.

They looked around nervously, glancing up and down the isolated streets. Duggan hurried over towards the distressed insect.

'Don't move a muscle… it will only make it worse,' Bongo spoke with an air of authority. He had studied web design for two years at school.

The ant stiffened, afraid to breathe. 'But help me… help me, please, before they come.' His pitiful cries echoed around the deserted streets.

'Hey, I've seen you before,' Bongo said. 'Didn't you score the winning goal in the big ant football game on the sands last week?'

'Yes…. It was me. I scored a hat-trick that day.' The ant's smiled, but it soon disappeared as he added, 'Quick! Hurry up and get me out of here.'

Unfortunately, before Bongo had chance to dismount off his taxi ride, they heard the stomp of boots coming from the next street. Duggan tried to back into the shadow of a lamp-post, but he was seen.

Twelve banana spiders appeared menacingly from out of nowhere. Uncle Paddy and Bongo ducked deep down into the rat's matted fur.

One soldier barked orders in a foreign language. He was astride a beetle, riding him like a horse. The others, who were on foot, proceeded to untangle the screaming ant from the web. Bongo watched as they fully immersed the terrified insect, in fresh web-spit and then strapped him to a woodlouse that was being used as some kind of pack mule.

The spider, on his beetle horse, looked suspiciously at the rat. Duggan stood perfectly still during the capture and imprisonment of the poor ant. A wide smile was frozen to his lips.

'What should I do?' the rat whispered through clenched teeth towards Bongo and Uncle Paddy.

'Play dumb.... And don't say a word,' Bongo replied, knowing fully well that playing dumb was not a problem to Duggan. It was getting him to stay quiet long enough for them to get out of there, that was what worried the spider most.

'What are you doing here?' the officer spoke in broken English.

The rodent shrugged his shoulders, nearly dislodging his two passengers from their hiding place.

The soldier yelled some more commands and pointed wildly.

Four spiders carrying razor-sharp pine-cones edged cautiously towards the rat.

'Search... search.' The spider on the beetle-back commanded.

All at once, the four spiders shuttled up each of Duggan legs. It tickled him, but he thought better of laughing out aloud. They started to rummage thoroughly through every inch of fur, prodding his skin with their sharp weapons.

Bongo and Uncle Paddy were hiding up by Duggan's neck. They tried to make themselves as small as possible. They held their breath as one of the searching guards scrabbled around only an inch away from them.

Bongo could feel a cough building up in his throat. Duggan was sweating. The stupid grin was still lodged firmly on his face.

The spider in charge sneered at him; his evil eyes pierced his soul. Duggan smile grew even wider.

One of the spiders in the search party was within touching distance of the fugitives. Uncle Paddy was ready to spring out and start swinging, even if he was minus his famous slugging leg.

They were suddenly saved when the booby-trap web over by the drainpipe started to shake violently. Again orders were barked out by the spider in charge.

The four banana spiders dismounted from the rat's body and they trooped off towards Centipede City, dragging the slave woodlouse and the cocooned ant (who was still wearing his lucky football boots) behind them.

'That was damn close,' said Bongo, trying to climb down off the creature.

'Pity about that.' Uncle Paddy flexed his muscles. 'I was looking forward to a good old punch up.'

'There will be more to come, Uncle…. Lots more.' He wished that that was a lie, but he knew that it was true, if they were to overcome these evil spiders.

On the other hand, Duggan couldn't speak at all. That was comforting news as far as the other two were concerned.

Bongo was coughing. His chest felt as if a large rhinoceros beetle was sitting on it; it was scary. He longed to see his mother, his father, his brother, and Greeneyez. Even Eric, the bright orange cross-dressing slow-worm, would have been a welcome face at this moment, even if it was plastered in make-up and lipstick.

Bongo again just felt like running away. Running far away to another part of the city where there wouldn't be any signs of the black spiders and their evil master.

He couldn't believe that only yesterday he had taken Greeneyez on the date of his life, and now all this was happening. He didn't like these banana spiders, their blackness, the coldness in their eyes, the voices, the strange and aggressive words and, worst of all, their total disregard for Dublin's insect life.

But, way down in the pit of his stomach, he knew that running away was no good. Today it was the docklands, tomorrow, Dublin, then what next? How far did a spider need to go to hid from these creatures of evil?

He also had a feeling inside that this was his fate. He realised that it was up to him, his Uncle Paddy, Duggan the tailless Rat, and anybody else they could find on their quest to win back Tiger-Moth Bay. He knew he needed to be strong if they were going to rescue the entire population of creepy-crawlies (including the woodlice) and rid this town of the evil Emperor and his henchmen.

As Bongo fell into a daydream about becoming the hero of Dublin and marrying Greeneyez, Duggan sneezed all over him.

'Duggan,' screamed Bongo and tried to hit him.

'I need a drink.' Uncle Paddy said, getting to his feet.

He completely forgot about his missing leg, and tripped off the rats back, landing on the floor with a thump.

Duggan started to laugh and banged his head on some iron railings. He crouched up in a ball.

Bongo stared at his Uncle, laying flat out on the floor, and Duggan, hopping around like a scolded cat and he hoped that they would bump into some friendly insects, and soon. Bongo announced, 'Let's go to Sam's Place… it will be relatively safe there… unless, of course, Sticky Licky is looking for some male company.'

Chapter 14

'Falling apart at the seams'

'Well! How do I look?' Emperor Balasz asked, his sinister eyes staring at the aptly named 'Second-Lieutenant for Making the Emperor Feel Good', (or Chief Creepy-Crawler), as the rest of the war cabinet referred to him.

'At least three skins younger your Highness. There's not a wrinkle to be seen on your face,' the Second-lieutenant commented, quickly making sure that Bollo, with his new crab claw weapon, wasn't sneaking up behind his back.

The Second-Lieutenant was relieved to see that the bodyguard was sitting on a chair at the back of the room, sharpening a vicious looking set of knuckle-dusters.

'I feel like a brand new spider today,' the Emperor announced. 'I feel so alive....full of vitality.'

He twirled about, his beetle cloak flowing freely about his shoulders.

Things had become considerably more pleasant about the palace since the Emperor had got his legs on the life-saving 'Belt of Kings'.

During that time it had not left his side for one second. He had worn it, constantly rubbed it, occasionally kissed it, and frequently licked it. To be truthful, there wasn't anything with an 'it' at the end of it that he hadn't done with it.

As he twisted and turned like a dancer performing some routine, the 'Second-lieutenant for Making the Emperor Feel Good' noticed a small section of dry skin falling away from the emperor's third left leg from the front. He wisely kept his observations to himself.

He was not alone; most of the rest of the cabinet had also seen it. Many sets of eyes looked at one another nervously. The only two to have missed the piece of skin landing on the floor was Bollo the bodyguard and the Emperor himself.

All present in the room, at one time or another, had witnessed the terrible mood swings that Emperor Balasz could fall into, especially when things were not going his way.

Once, back in his country of birth, he had an entire village of mosquitoes massacred without mercy, after he had found his first grey pubic hair. Or the occasion when he had dreamt that his mother and his family were planning to murder him. That night, just before the sun had risen, he, allegedly, smothered his mother with a fluffy pillow, whilst giving instructions to have his brothers and sisters imprisoned in the dungeons of doom, and tortured. It was a place that no one ever returned from, unless in a tight-fitted cocooned coffin.

Back in the war room, the Emperor was too busy prancing about to detect the dead skin coming away from his body. Luckily, one of the guards kicked it under the table before it was seen.

'I feel great,' the Emperor announced. 'Give me the biggest whacking stick in the box,' he pointed to his bodyguard, 'I'm going to beat that Terry the woodlouse mayor with it for a while.'

He skipped out of the room whistling a tuneless tune. The members of his war cabinet breathed a collective sigh of relief... for the time being anyway.

Anthony Bunko

Chapter 15

'The plot gets thicker'

Bongo and Uncle Paddy sat in Sam's Place feeling safe amongst the supposed freak creatures of nature, and the so-called monsters of insect society.

The unlikely heroes had been there for a while and were indulging themselves in several well deserved cold beers before continuing on the dangerous journey to face their destiny.

Duggan, who again hadn't been able to squeeze up the narrow crevice-way to the cemetery of misfits, had been despatched to snoop about and see what information he could find out.

Uncle Paddy was just about getting to grips with losing his prized weapon that had been his right slugging leg. To prove some point or other, he decided to climb up onto the bar and attempt to do as many press-ups as he could do with only seven legs. Every time he reached the milestone of a new one hundred press-ups, rounds of drinks were supplied to all the regulars, complements of the tongue-less Welsh caterpillar with the large head.

While Uncle Paddy showed off his strength, Bongo again found himself in deep conversation with the cross-dressing slow-worm, who sat opposite in a brightly coloured, off the shoulder, orange evening gown.

Bongo didn't know if it was the effects of the alcohol, but Eric was starting to look rather attractive, in a 'slow-worm disguised as an earwig' type of way. The teenage spider eventually put it down to the effects of the drink and the poor lighting in the bar.

'So what did you say was going on out in Tiger-Moth Bay?' Eric asked, sipping a rainbow coloured cocktail that had a blade of grass sticking out of the side of the glass.

'An army of killer banana spiders, lead by some evil Emperor called Bal-hash, has stolen the 'Belt of Kings', imprisoned all our families in large tea-chests and worst of all, they killed my brother.' Tears rolled down his cheeks, spilling onto the bar.

'I'm so sorry… banana spiders… you say. Stolen the 'Belt of Kings', tea-chests, murder…. Whatever next? It makes you glad we've got a place like this to come to.' They both glanced simultaneously around the crypt. Never in his short life had Bongo heard truer words spoken.

'But this is not my world,' Bongo suddenly thought to himself, spying a suspicious looking cockroach entering the bar. The insect was wearing a nasty scar across his face. 'My world is out there, my family, my girl-fly. It's up to me to save this city.'

There was a small disruption as the tongue-less Welsh caterpillar with the large head proceeded to throw the cockroach, with the nasty scar across his face, back out the same way as he had just come in.

'Banned, is he?' Eric asked the bartender gingerly.

'Mmmmmrg…mmmmrg…mrrg,' the tongue-less Welsh caterpillar with the large head replied, before nipping off to serve someone at the other end of the bar.

Bongo was amazed by the sheer fact that no matter what strange and bizarre thing took place in this establishment, no one really took a blind bit of notice. Except the blind moth, who would actually raise his head but couldn't see what was going on anyway.

'Is that a new costume?' Bongo asked

'Brand spanking new! Fresh off the peg this morning. My tailor is a genius!' Eric stood up and spun around.

The sound of wolf-whistles filled the smoky bar at the sight of the slow-worm doing a twirl in the middle of the room.

Of course, the tongue-less Welsh caterpillar with the large head, was unable to join in due to the fact that one normally needed a tongue to make the whistling noise. So, instead, he happily clanked some glasses together and did his usual wild jig.

'Who's your tailor?' Bongo nonchalantly asked the slow-worm.

The spider was only looking to engage the slow-worm in some meaningless small-talk, until he sobered up enough to hatch a plan to rescue his family and his girl-fly.

'Mr Zimmermann, the silk-worm, made it for me. He can make a silk purse out of a woodlouse's ear.'

Again, the slow-worm had caused an explosion of laughter, as they all turned to stare at the comical figure of an old woodlouse that had been born with ears the size of fruit bats, sitting in the corner.

'Shut-up you freak,' the big bat-eared woodlouse cried at Eric, before storming off to the toilets.

Bongo shook his head, wondering if he'd ever get out of this bar and into normality again.

As he watched the tongue-less Welsh caterpillar accidentally fall off the bar landing on his large head, the teenage spider suddenly had a brainwave or a bolt of lightening, or whatever the term is to explain when a young teenage spider has an idea. His eyes lit up the gloom like a lighthouse illuminating the coastline on a foggy March morning.

With all the excitement of recent days he'd forgotten that most of the worm species didn't reside down on the dockside of Tiger-Moth Bay. He had been told by his dad that it was something to do with the salt in the air. Apparently it frizzled their skins, which meant that most of the worm fraternity were not locked in tea-chests in the warehouse, but were probably alive and well and living over by the Westside, in the grassy knoll patch where the big, brown wooden things reach up towards the big blue thing that the birds fly in.

'Uncle Paddy.... Uncle Paddy. I have a plan to get our family, our city and my girl-fly back, before the white flakes of snow come,' Bongo yelled, rushing over to a table where Uncle Paddy was arm-wrestling a gigantic two-headed dragonfly, with a bad attitude and even badder breath.

The dragonfly snarled at the young spider.

'Quick Uncle, we have got to go.' Bongo ignored the stare from the insect. 'But firstly we need to capture one of those banana spiders.'

There was a sound of snapping, as Uncle Paddy, viciously tore the dragonfly's arm in two. 'Sorry Victor...don't know my own strength.' He stared at the limb that swung lifeless in his powerful leg, before handing the stump back to the poor dragonfly.

Uncle Paddy then turned to Bongo and said 'If we catch one of those slimy banana spider creatures... can I beat it up?

'If you must,' Bongo replied, still staring at the sight of the two-headed dragonfly who was trying to reattach the piece of arm to the flailing stump.

Bongo noticed that one of the heads of the dragonfly had fainted and flopped to its side.

'Can I bruise him….? Can I batter him…? Can I…?' Uncle Paddy continued.

'You can do what you like, but we need to take him to see Mr Zimmermann, the silk-worm, first.'

'Mr Zimmermann…. Doesn't he run a Butterfly opium den over by the Iron Bridge?' Uncle Paddy innocently mentioned.

Both Bongo and Eric the cross-dressing slow-worm glanced at the old street-fighter.

'I don't think so Uncle. He's a costume maker.'

'Are you sure?'

'Yes…he made that earwig costume for Eric here,' Bongo informed his uncle.

Uncle Paddy looked at Eric, then back to his nephew, then whispered, 'Aaaaah…so he's not an earwig then?' He rudely pointed to the creature in the orange.

'No, he's a slow-worm, Uncle.'

'Well I'll go to the foot of my stairs! I was sure he was an earwig.' Uncle Paddy shook Eric's hand. 'Nice to meet you. Did you know I once knew an earwig who wanted to be a slow-worm? Small insect world ain't it!'

Bongo had decided that they had squandered enough time. 'Quick Uncle, we have no time to hang about. I'll explain the plan as we go.'

Bongo reached for his cap.

They rushed out through the graveyard, passed the one-legged war veteran and the ladybirds, out through the dark passageway and met up with Duggan yet again.

The three make-shift heroes sat on a doorstep. The teenage spider spelt out the first part of his plan. Bongo had decided to only give the plan to them in small, manageable doses, otherwise, Duggan would be completely confused by the amount of detail or, worse still, blab it to someone that he shouldn't.

Several moments elapsed before anyone spoke.

'But why me?' Duggan cried at them. 'Why have I got to be the decoy? I can't stand the feel of webbing and those hairy black spiders really give me the creeps.'

'Look Duggan… brave, brave Duggan,' Bongo diplomatically added. 'We've got to capture one of them. It's no good one of us pretending to get caught in the web…. Spiders can't stick to web-spit, we have non-web stick skin, so they will know there's something not right.'

Duggan nervously scratched his ears. 'OK, but what have I got to do again?'

'You pretend to be tangled up in the booby-trap web. When they come to release you…wham…we nab one of them,' Bongo explained positively.

Duggan eventually decided to carry out the first part of the plan, but only when the other two agreed never to leave the rat alone again.

So the scene was set. Duggan wrapped his leg up in the silk thread over by the rusty railings near the brewery.

On Bongo's signal, the rat shook his leg violently.

Within seconds a swarm of about ten soldier spiders descended on the rodent. Only difference this time compared to when the ant had been caught, was that all the banana spiders were now riding on the backs of poor beetles.

Duggan had seen them coming from way off in the distance. He closed his eyes tightly; otherwise he would have probably run away into the fading light.

The same spider that was in charge earlier in the day looked at the rat with contempt, and spat on the ground. He wished he had been authorised to dispose of the hairy, germ-infested rodent, but he was under strict instructions not to.

The Emperor had told them all in his 'Achieving World Domination' address to his army that firstly, they had to conquer the insects, secondly the rodents, followed quickly by those disgusting lazy cats, then who knows, perhaps even the giants themselves.

The spider in charge knew that Emperor Balasz was slightly insane, to put it mildly. But he also realised that being able to travel around the world, riding on the back of pitiful creatures and torturing defenceless insects was miles better than working for a living. Back in the rainforest of South America, he had been a cook in a spider fast-fly-food establishment, getting paid two grubs a month.

'Not you again,' the spider shouted at the rat. He instructed two spiders to free the irritating rodent.

They dismounted as the other spiders' scuttled back to base camp, racing each other on their beetles to see who could get there the fastest.

Bongo and Uncle Paddy watched from behind an empty paint container that lay amongst some rubbish.

'Are you ready?' Bongo took a deep breath and went to stand up.

Uncle Paddy placed his strong leg on the young insect's chest. 'Leave it to me my boy, this won't take long.' He sauntered out into the clearing.

The daddy long-legs coughed.

It wasn't a hearty cough, or a cough that indicated that someone was suffering from the sickness, it was more a 'turn around and see who's behind you' type of cough from the back of his throat.

The soldiers spun around simultaneously and reached for their weapons, but Uncle Paddy was ready and itching to bash some of those nasty big-headed bully spider's about a bit.

A jab from his left, an undercut from his second right, a sharp knee in the crouch and a flying head-butt later, and the two soldiers lay unconscious, sleeping with the stars.

Bongo was impressed. It may not have been strictly Queensbury rules, but this wasn't a boxing ring. This was the streets and these streets were now occupied by evil. The only way to overcome evil was to fight fire with fire.

Duggan, still stuck in the web, clapped triumphantly. 'Bravo, Mr Dacey, bravo.'

They quickly went to work. They bound both of the banana spiders up in web-spit and threw one of them on the back of the rat. The other was hidden out of the way underneath a small pebble by a cast iron fence.

Bongo and Uncle Paddy climbed on board the rodent, and Duggan raced off towards the other side of town to carry out phase two of Bongo's extraordinary four-step plan.

Chapter 16

'Costume changes'

It took Duggan and his three passengers two hours to reach the patch of grass where most of the worms hung out.

Although there were no signs of banana spiders beyond the confines of the docks, there were many other dangers lurking throughout these dark, unfamiliar streets.

Of course the giants still offered the greatest threat, especially the ones with the dirty ingrained faces, who earned their living from catching rats, skinning them, and selling their meat to the rum taverns to put in something called Dublin pies.

There was always a healthy profit in the rat trade, so the streets and gutter ways were always alive with ambushes, traps and snares.

To make matters worse, and a lot more dangerous, there were the cats. The cats were constantly hunting for something to either eat or just to play with when they got bored.

Duggan may well have been the hero of the scrap of Baker Alleyway, but he certainly kept his eyes peeled, and his claws on maximum alert during this journey.

The rat decided to take the back, back streets, where even the shadows stuck together in greater numbers. He occasionally ducked down the sewage system, or darted up a drainpipe on hearing the slightest noise.

Up on his back, Uncle Paddy was practicing punching with his left leg. His target was the head of the unfortunate banana spider that was repeatedly knocked out cold every time he tried to wake up.

Bongo didn't speak much.

He used the time to think. He was worried about the wellbeing of his family, and he was longing to see Greeneyez once again. He also wished his brother was still alive. He would have known exactly what to do in order to get them out of this situation. He would have already hatched a simple, but effective, plan by now, one that would have disposed of the hairy black spiders and that slimy, evil Emperor.

Bongo knew it was no good looking back, he had a lot to live up to, and deep down he wasn't quite sure if he could do it. Only time would tell.

They finally reached their destination, just as the moon was beginning to show its knowing smile over the top of the horizon, between the space where the two big blue things touched.

The gang asked several worms for directions to the tailor's workshop, but without receiving much success in the form of replies.

It was difficult enough to get anyone to actually speak to Bongo and his companions, because worms believed, rightly or wrongly, that they were the superior creatures in the universe. They thought that they alone were more important than any other species, including the giant people.

The idea was originated by the great worm philosopher, Gerald La Scaly-belly, who wrote a best selling book entitled 'God and his Twelve Earth Worms.... The Defining Years.'

So, because of this perceived superior attitude, the questions from the unlikely heroes were greeted with a wall of silence by the wriggling insects.

Bongo eventually got the information he desperately required, when Uncle Paddy, with his bare hands, held an earth-worm in a head-lock, and threatened him with the mother-of-all snakebites, if he didn't tell them what they needed to know and fast.

The distressed, slithering insect, still in a leg-grip, led them to the front door of the costume designer. It turned out to be a hole in one of the large brown wooden things, the entrance covered in foliage. They searched around and finally discovered a camouflaged front door.

Bongo knocked and they waited impatiently.

They could hear someone puffing and panting on the other side of the bark. With a noisy creak the door was slowly pulled inwards. Mr Zimmermann squinted through his spectacles at the three unfamiliar faces and quickly tried to shut the door again.

'Aaarrhh.' Duggan let out a yell as his snout, unintentionally prevented the heavy wooden door being closed tightly.

'There is nothing for you here.... I am just an old silk-worm with my sewing machine... go away.'

'Brilliant!' Bongo spoke first, as they barged past the bespectacled grey haired old silk-worm.

Once inside the tree, they made themselves comfortable in the small, but practical lounge area. It was a tight squeeze for the rodent but he was never getting left outside again.

'Hey... what do you think you are doing? You just can't barge into someone's home... especially in Cree-season,' the silk-worm grunted scornfully.

His expression soon changed after he took one look at Uncle Paddy's frown. The worm decided to keep his mouth closed as he slumped down onto a chair, waiting his fate.

'Mr Zimmermann,' Bongo again spoke.

He was increasingly becoming the spokes-spider for this small group, which wasn't totally unexpected, since his Uncle Paddy was punch-drunk from years of boxing and rum, and could only mutter the odd word or two. While, on the other hand, Duggan could talk the hind leg off a donkey. Unfortunately, most of what he said was lies, or rubbish, or a rich mixture of both.

Mr Zimmermann was obviously taken aback and very confused with the familiarity the young spider had with his name. He nodded his head in acknowledgment, his body was shaking. The piece of chalk that was positioned behind his ear fell to the ground.

Bongo continued, 'Mr Zimmermann, before we go on would you like a drink?'

'I'd love one?' Uncle Paddy answered for him, and skittered in the kitchen to find some.

Bongo could see many costumes and disguises hanging on hooks behind him. He wondered if the little orange earwig sailor outfit was made for who he thought it was.

'Mr Zimmermann, this is a matter of life and death.' Bongo then went on to explain in great detail the events of the last week in Tiger-moth Bay.

The spider was only interrupted twice. The first was when his uncle handed everyone a stiff drink. The second was when Duggan jumped in to ask the tailor if he knew who he was going out with.

When Bongo had finished the story, the clothes designer necked his drink and took a long drag on a pipe. He removed his little round glasses, before speaking.

'But that's all fine and dandy, and I'm really concerned for all the insects down on the docks, but what is all this to do with me?'

This was a simple question, to which both Uncle Paddy and Duggan didn't have an answer. Up to this point, Bongo hadn't disclosed that part of the plan to them yet.

'Mr Zimmermann, we need you to make us some banana soldier spider costumes so we can dress up in disguise.'

'OK! I see… you want me to make you some banana soldier spider costumes just like that. There's been no please or thank you. You didn't even wipe your feet when you barged into my home. So, as far as I am concerned, you can find yourself another tailor.'

'But we need your help Mr Zimmermann,' Bongo pleaded.

The silk-worm looked at the teenager, then at Uncle Paddy who was flexing his muscles. The worm added: 'But even if I could do it, I couldn't possible start them until at least….' The silk-worm started flicking through his diary. 'Hang on. I have a wedding dress and bridesmaid costumes to make for Shelia the tapeworm's daughter's wedding. Sixty four uniforms for a traditional ants' jazz band who are marching in the sunnytime pageant on Saturday, and a couple of ballroom gowns for Eric the cross-dresser. So let me see.'

He started to do some calculations in his head. The other three watched him intently.

'So I could maybe start them, at the best case, ncxt Tuesday and it would probably take me about a week to get them finished.'

'Sorry Mr Zimmermann… we need them sooner,' Bongo replied, the tone of his voice getting louder and more aggressive.

'How much sooner?' Mr Zimmermann asked, aware that the mood in the room was turning a little aggressive.

'What about the 'We need them tomorrow morning,' kind of sooner?'

The silk-worm coughed and spluttered. He replaced his glasses back on his nose and chuckled.

A thick cloud of smoke escaped from his pipe. 'Tomorrow…? tomorrow…? that's impossible. It can't be done. And anyway, I don't even know what these banana spiders look like. Have you got a sketch?' He knew that spider's were useless at sketching. Apparently they had difficulty in holding chalk or pencils in their pads.

A smile ran across the silk-worm's face

But it soon ran straight off again when Bongo mentioned that they had something much better than a sketch. At this point, Uncle Paddy reached into the matted hair of the rodent and plucked out a gagged, and slightly dazed banana spider.

'Oh that's why we needed to capture one of the spiders,' Duggan thought, but kept his observations to himself.

Mr Zimmermann was enthralled by the strange insect placed in front of him.

He walked around the prisoner, poking and prodding the skin of the creature. He marvelled at its intricate design. He had never witnessed skin with such a hairy, but shiny texture. And its blackness was blacker than he had imagined possible.

'So what do you think?' Bongo could see the delight in the silk-worm's eyes. He knew he had the designer hooked.

'Magnificent! The layers! The colour! The design!' The silk-worm was drooling from the mouth, but cautiously added 'Even if I could drop everything else... it would take me a couple of days to copy and...'

Bongo stood up irritated and yelled, 'Look we don't have a couple of days... all the insects are going to be packed off to their death... don't you understand? I thought worms were supposed to be the intelligent ones!'

'Yeah!' said Uncle Paddy

'Yeah yeah!' copied Duggan, unsure what he was 'Yeah-yeahing' about.

'Well you need to find yourself another designer in that case,' the silk-worm was adamant, refusing to budge.

Bongo could feel Duggan and Uncle Paddy looking to him for guidance.

'Should I knock his teeth out?' Uncle Paddy whispered, not so quietly to his nephew.

Bongo shook his head. Whatever happened he needed the silk-worm fit and well. He wondered what is brother would have done in this tricky situation. He walked around the compact room, giving himself time to consider his options.

He noticed a photograph hanging over the fireplace. It was a black and white snapshot that showed Mr Zimmermann sitting on his chair with all his nephews bouncing on his long body.

Bongo smiled before uttering the words that squeezed out from his mouth, 'How are the nephews Mr Zimmermann? I bet they are a nice juicy age by now.' He winked at his Uncle Paddy and Duggan before adding menacingly, 'Are you hungry boys… because I'm famished…I could eat a ….' Bongo glared at the photograph.

He could see the horror appear on the silk-worms face.

'Ok…! Ok! I'll have two costumes ready by the morning… but leave my nephews alone.' The worm wriggled about uncomfortably.

Bongo looked up to the big blue thing, hoping his brother was looking down and was suitably impressed with his little brother's newly acquired persuasive skills.

'But what about me? Duggan interrupted, 'I wanna costume… you said that you wouldn't leave me again.'

'It's OK Duggan…. I promise we won't leave you. You will be the centre of the entire operation.'

Duggan didn't know if being the centre of the entire operation was good or bad. He smiled meekly as he saw Uncle Paddy dragging the banana spider, by his feet, into the sewing workshop.

Anthony Bunko

Chapter 17

'The banana skins'

Sprawled out in front of a roaring tree fire, the teenage spider, the street-wise daddy long-legs and the tailless, talkative rat sat up for most of the night, sampling something that smelt like rum but tasted like dandelions. They told stories whilst Mr Zimmermann beavered away on his sewing machine in the other room.

Uncle Paddy's was on top form, and enlightened them all with his street fighting tales which concluded with the day he had won his famous boxing match with Gizzy, the Great Grasshopper. Duggan, as usual, was trying his best to match the ex-street fighting spider, story for story, tall tale for taller tales.

The rat was in the middle of telling them about the terrible night that a giant moth had bitten his tail clean off, when Uncle Paddy challenged him.

'I thought you told me yesterday that your tail was pulled off by a pack of alley-cat.' The old street fighter poured some more rum into his glass.

'Who told you that rubbish? I've never said such a thing. It was a moth, I'm telling you, a huge moth with a set of gnashers that wouldn't have been out of place in the mouth of a deranged pony.'

Bongo had heard it all before, but was more than happy just to sit back and listen to the other two racketeers verbally fight it out.

At around about the time of night when most insects would be tucked up in their warm bed dreaming about this and that and sometimes the other, the tailor emerged into the dimly lit room shaking his head and tutting profusely. His worn tape measure was draped around his neck, his hands were covered in white chalk.

'What's wrong?' Bongo asked, sensing that something was bothering the silk-worm.

'It's the model you've got me.' He paced back and forth, fiddling with his specs. His shoulders hunched over in deep thought. He slammed his old tape measure onto the surface of the table.

'Is he playing up?' Uncle Paddy grunted, rising up from his chair.

They all glanced at the soldier who was bound, gagged, and laid out on the tailor's cutting table, eyes bulging wide. The prisoner's only thought was how he could escape from the daddy long-legs.

'No, he's not playing up. It's just that he's too…. too much alive, he's too real.' He slumped down onto the settee. 'He's too…. whole.'

Bongo looked at the other two. Confusion was written in large letters over all of their faces. This was especially true with Duggan the rat who was still trying to figure out what the slow-worm was doing with a model instead of the banana spider in the first place.

'We don't understand Mr Zimmermann: what do you actually want?' Bongo yet again asked the question for all of them.

'It would be so much easier if he was…. how can I put this?' The silk-worm searched for the right words. He took a shot of dandelion rum. 'If he was sort of …. dead.'

'Dead!' the three shouted in unison.

'Mmmrggg,' the banana spider muttered through the gag, rolling about violently.

The banana spider prisoner may have been from the other side of the world, but a word like 'dead' was universally understood, whatever country one came from.

He rolled to his left and rocked to his right and eventually fell off the table with a loud thud, knocking himself out yet again. At least this time it wasn't with the help of Uncle Paddy's left leg.

'Yeah, dead,' the silk-worm muttered extremely seriously, 'and then preferably skinned.'

'Dead and then… skinned,' the rat mouthed the words to himself.

Bongo was not quite sure what the tailor was barking on about, but what he did know was that all this talking was eating in to the short amount of time that they had left.

'Look Mr Zimmermann… why would he be better dead and skinned?'

'You see I could then trace around the pattern and I would finish in double quick time.'

Uncle Paddy stood up immediately, 'Oh… why the hell didn't you just tell us that in the first place.' He wiped some jam off the corner of his grinning mouth and added, 'I'll be back in a minute.' The street fighter entered the little workshop. His big frame disappeared as he kicked the door closed.

Back in the front room, no one said a word. Even Duggan's tongue was tied firmly shut. The clock on the wall was the only thing that dared to make a noise. Its second hand ticked loudly. They all stared, silently counting down the seconds.

Then right on cue, at exactly fifty-nine seconds precisely, Uncle Paddy appeared, holding aloft the peeled skin of the banana spider.

'Well that was much easier than I thought?' He threw the suit over Mr Zimmermann's head and as he sat back down on a comfortable chair, he added, to the amazement of his nephew, 'Did I tell you about that time I fought a gypsy cockroach for the vacant British title in a wheat field in Kent.'

The silk-worm didn't hang around to hear the fascinating tale from the daddy long-legs. The worm dashed off with the banana spider skin, leaving Bongo and Duggan speechless, and in complete awe of the one time 'insect boxing Champion of the World.'

Bongo reached for the dandelion rum and poured them all a large drink.

Much later, as the darkness thinned and the morning started to shine through the gaps in the door, the three supposed heroes of Dublin's Tiger-Moth Bay slept, as the sound of the sewing machine buzzed away furiously.

Much, much later, Duggan opened one eye. He could hear a loud snoring and wheezing sound coming from the direction of the armchair by the fire, where the old street fighting spider lay fast asleep, dreaming of past glories, buckets full of rum and Sticky Licky.

The rat put his paws to his ears and turned his back on the noisy spider.

Suddenly, he stiffened, afraid to make the slightest noise. He rubbed his eyes in disbelief. 'Was he seeing things?' he thought, because there, tiptoeing around the room, was a banana spider. He was almost too scared to believe it, but it was true; he could see it.

Without considering his actions, Duggan leapt up in one movement, landing on the creature and pinned him solidly to the floor.

'I've caught one.... quick Bongo... I've caught one. He was surely trying to kill us,' the rat wailed at the top of his voice.

'Duggan… Duggan,' a familiar voice came from way inside the banana spider that was getting squashed under the weight of the vermin.

'Duggan… it's me…. you tailless idiot. Its Bongo…. Now get off you big lump of lard, before you break the suit and I get Uncle Paddy on to you.'

The rat instantly rolled off.

Bongo, who was actually inside the banana spider costume, got up on three knees, gasping for air. Over by the workshop door, Mr Zimmermann stood smiling to himself, holding up another costume in triumph.

'If I must say so myself, it's not bad for my first attempt, and all made from an old leather boot, a couple of raisins, and a spot or two of coal soot.'

Uncle Paddy continued to sleep through the commotion, feeling slightly drunk from all that rum which was swilling around in his dreams.

Chapter 18

'Things turn flaky'

The deafening shriek that came bellowing out from the Emperor's master bedroom made everyone's gooey blood run cold.

Seconds later, there was further commotion as several of the Emperor's harem of lady spiders came scurrying out of the bedroom door, followed by four pairs of slippers, which had been thrown in anger in all directions.

The war council of banana spiders was already assembled around the table. They were all extremely nervous. Most of them were afraid and some of them were literately scared to death in the knowledge that something bad was about to happen to at least one of them. They all held on tightly to the armrests of their chairs. Their knuckles of their pads were white with anxiety.

The insects all jumped in one big mass, as if joined together at the hip, when Emperor Balasz came scampering into the room.

Balasz was draped in the royal dressing gown and had an expression on his thin face that spread fear and caused all of their knees to knock. The many sets of spider eyes immediately found a convenient space on the floor. They refused to look in his direction.

Unusually the Emperor had been in a good mood for the last few days but they all realised that it wouldn't last; they could sense that a storm was brewing inside of him. But, more importantly, they wondered which one of them would end up getting caught in the eye of the Emperor's hurricane.

'It's the lull before the storm,' someone had mentioned as they all sat in silence, terror written all over their faces.

The spider who felt that he had the most to fear and dread, was the 'Second-lieutenant for Making the Emperor Feel Good.' He found himself shaking in his eight boots.

Whilst on the other hand, (or leg), the only one to feel reasonably safe in the current climate was the 'First Lady Commander for Finding Things,' who sat back relaxed, powdering her face and smirking.

She had successfully carried out her assignment in the required timescale demanded by the evil tyrant. She had not only found the famous 'Belt of Kings', (agreed only with the help of those deliciously tasting French snails), but she had also discovered, and had redecorated, the magnificent palace, where they were all seated that morning.

So, all-in-all, she felt quite pleased with herself and found her new role much more rewarding and exciting than being in charge of inventing new web designs, which, to be honest, hadn't really changed in appearance or structure since Egyptian times.

The Emperor glided around the room. 'Hey you…. the village clown.' He pointed his long bony toes menacingly towards the 'Second-lieutenant for Making Him Feel Good'. 'How old do I look this morning?'

Before the 'Second lieutenant for Making Him Feel Good' could answer, the Emperor added chillingly, 'and I suggest you take a long hard look before you supply me with your answer.'

The Emperor's red eyes were as cold as ice; imaginary icicles hang from his eyelids.

The Second-lieutenant hesitated for a spilt second and slumped down lower in his seat.

He puffed out his cheeks; sweat ran like a river down his back, nestling under his many leg-pits. He could almost feel the big grey cloud of doom positioning itself above his head. He thought, 'Why didn't I just stay back home and work in my granddad's novelty joke shop like my brothers.'

'Well, I'm waiting.' The Emperor tapped his tiny toes on the table.

'At least….. two or three skins younger…your Highness…. at least that… if not more.' His little Adams apple protruded like he had just swallowed a double maggot sandwich with an extra portion of ants' blood.

The Emperor scuttled up and stood right in front of him. His dressing gown flapped open. 'I'll ask you again; how old do I look this morning?' The sudden loudness in his voice even sent a chill down the spine of the 'old fishing boat turned upside down' palace that they were in.

'Definitely two, three, or maybe.... four skins younger. You look great.... just like a spiderling.... honest.' He started to sound less convincing each time he opened his mouth.

The 'First Lady Commander for Finding Things' sat polishing her nails and fluttering her false eyelashes.

When the poor spider had finished answering the loaded question, he closed his eyes, waiting in anticipation to hear the foot pads of Bollo, the bodyguard, trotting up behind him, crab claw ready and uncocked.

'Well if I look that bloody good... what the hell is this then?' The Emperor slammed a dead piece of moulted skin onto the table. It caused everyone's bums to leave the seat. The 'Second-lieutenant for Making the Emperor Feel Good,' started to cry. Tears slalomed down his pitiful face and shoot off his chin, landing way down on his chest. The 'First Lady Commander for Finding Things,' tried unsuccessfully, to hide her grin.

The poor spider tried to speak but no words would force themselves out of his mouth. He found himself in a verbal corner, without the strength of speech to get him out. The ground appeared to open up under his eight feet and started to suck him in.

The Emperor held up his front leg, which instantly caused the usual hush to cover the room in a flash.

'I'm not asking you,' Balasz yelled at the shaking insect that was now down on his knees, sobbing and pleading for his head not to be popped. 'I'm talking to her.' The Emperor's toes pointed across the table.

The rest of the spiders slowly raised their eyes up to face their leader. To their great relief they found that the Emperor was staring and pointing at the 'First Lady Commander for Finding Things.'

The grin on her face fell to the floor, along with a set of false eyelashes.

'I… I… I….' She couldn't quite comprehend what was going on.

The Emperor decided to fill in the missing gaps for her. 'You found me this damn useless belt, which doesn't work. You promised me that it would make me six skins younger and stop me moulting. You said that it would make me all powerful and feared throughout the world. So why hasn't it worked?…. Come on… I want answers.'

The 'First Lady Commander for Finding Things' knew that she hadn't said any of these things. In fact, the Emperor himself had actually said them. He had been the only one to believe the tale told to him by the trap-door spider back in his homeland.

Everyone else in the room also knew this, but there was no way that they would stick up for her.

She had become a right, spiteful, spider-bitch since she found the 'Belt of Kings.'

The First Lady was about to mention how well she had designed the master bedroom when the Emperor attacked.

He rarely did his own dirty work nowadays (especially in public) but today his blood was boiling. The thorn from the fresh rose bush pieced the 'First Lady Commander for Finding Things' heart. He twisted the sharp instrument until the rage that exploded inside of him, subsided.

The other sets of false eyelashes also fell from the dying lady-spider's eyes on to the floor.

Balasz wiped the blood off the thorn on the material of his dressing gown.

In one movement, he turned to face the 'Second-lieutenant for Making the Emperor Feel Good' (who was still hiding under the table) and chillingly uttered 'You ever lie to me again…. and I'll puck out your eyeballs.'

He threw the false eyelashes at the insect under the table and told him that he must wear them until they sailed back home. In an instant, the 'Second-lieutenant for Making the Emperor Feel Good' had staggered to his feet and started to attach the false eyelashes to his eyes. He realised that he may appear stupid to the rest of the war cabinet, but it was miles better than having his head popped.

The Emperor then pointed at a young apprentice work-spider, who had only come in to mend the dodgy heating system.

'Hey, you!'

'Yes your Highness?' the young apprentice replied. The monkey-wrench that he was holding shook uncontrollable in his leg.

'Come here! What's your name?'

'Trevo… your Highness. My name is Trevo.'

Then to everyone's surprise, (and joy) Emperor Balasz announced that the young apprentice was now the new 'Commander for Finding Things.'

All the other spiders clapped wildly (more out of relief that they hadn't been selected for the poisoned role than admiration for the young apprentice). Emperor Balasz threw him the badge which had his new job title printed on it. Some of the lettering was covered in blood.

'He may look good in blue dungarees, but wait until his head is clamped in Bollo's crab claw,' someone whispered, while nudging a colleague.

The rest of the war cabinet giggled.

The new ex-apprentice work-spider who had previously been responsible for ensuring that the Heating System was working, was chuffed at being promoted.

Sadly he was still too young and naive to fully appreciate why all the important spiders of the war cabinet were patting him on the back and wishing him luck so enthusiastically.

The Emperor raised his front leg yet again.

They all sat in silence, eyes staring back at the floor of the ship. No one dared look at his extra evil set of red eyes that glowed in the darkness.

He paced around, repeating the same question over and over again. 'Why doesn't it work...? What's wrong with it?'

The newly appointed 'Apprentice Commander for Finding Things' held up his leg, trying to attract the Emperor's attention.

The Emperor just stared at his newest recruit. His cheeks turned red with anger.

'Sorry Emperor, but do you believe that a stupid piece of old metal can really give anyone eternal life? Come on, lets be fair.' The apprentice was quite pleased with his first contribution in his new position.

The 'General for Telling the Truth,' also wanted to tell the Emperor this fact, but he was too much of a yellow-belly chicken to do that.

The Emperor strolled up to the new member of the round table and whispered, 'Look, I'm in a very bad mood. I'm falling apart, I'm surrounded by idiots and you still haven't fixed the bloody heating system. So unless you want me to instruct Bollo, over there, to stick that monkey-wrench where the sun doesn't shine, then I would be quiet for the moment... if I was you!'

The apprentice turned to see Bollo grinning back at him.

The Emperor turned to the big muscular bodyguard and told him to start transporting the tea-chests full of insects onto the banana ship. They would be sailing back to South America in the morning.

'We will feast until our bellies burst on our long journey home, and still have enough to feed my citizens back in our home country.' He clapped his hands and seven lady-spider's waltzed in carrying a grape and a hot towel.

Anthony Bunko

Chapter 19

'Terry the woodlouse is big leggy'

A sudden bout of muffled coughing rose up from over by the large fire place. Everyone in the room turned around to see who would have the nerve to make such a noise when the Emperor was holding court.

The war cabinet stared in amazement at the perpetrator of the coughing crime. There, dangling by the neck, over by the door, Terry the woodlouse was swinging from side to side, smiling as best he could under the circumstances.

Terry's hallucinations had become more obscure the longer he had hung there.

Now, he not only firmly believed that he was Erico the Spanish matador; he also insisted that he was a fully-trained belly-dancer as well. He wriggled his stomach in a rotational motion to try to prove the point. Again, this was a remarkable feat of the woodlouse's imagination, since he had never stepped foot outside Tiger-Moth Bay and didn't real know what a belly was, never mind that it could dance in the most particular way!

'Ain't that slimy thing dead yet?' the Emperor asked the 'Minister for Dishing Out Punishment.'

'It's his protective skin around his neck, your Highness.' The 'Minister for Dishing Out Punishment's' reply was extremely sheepish and low key.

Terry coughed again, swinging sufficiently enough to make eye contact with the Emperor.

'Well, if you couldn't kill him by hanging him, why didn't you do it some other way, then?' The Emperor left the question dangling there, just like Terry.

'Because you said to hang him up, your Highness.' The 'Minister for Dishing Out Punishments' said, now wishing he'd burnt and buried the damn ugly creature last week, as he had wanted to do.

'Am I surrounded by fools and idiots?' The Emperor was upset and threw a grape across the room. It hit Terry.

The Emperor then snatched the monkey-wrench out of the pocket of the newly appointed 'Apprentice Commander for Finding Things,' and whacked the 'Minister for Dishing Out Punishment,' over the head with it. The thud, as metal hit skin, sounded very painful and unpleasant.

Even Terry winced.

'I think the woodlouse has got something to say,' Bollo, the muscular bodyguard, interrupted.

'What do you mean he's got something to say?' The Emperor slithered across the shiny floor. 'I refuse point blank to communicate with that low-life... I have enough trouble getting through to you lot never mind things like that....now take it out the back and beat it to death with sticks and throw it in the sea.'

'But Emperor, perhaps it's trying to tell us about the belt?' the new 'Apprentice Commander for Finding Thing's piped up, to the great annoyance of the rest of the war cabinet, who had all thought the same thing, but had been to scared to say it.

Emperor Balasz summoned one of his henchmen to cut the creature down.

'And make sure that he falls on his head when you cut the cord,' he indicated to the soldiers.

Terry was immediately released from the noose. The guards made extra sure that he did land head first on the hard ground. This pleased the tyrant no end.

Emperor Balasz loomed large over the woodlouse before speaking, 'What do you know about the 'Belt of Kings', Fat Belly?'

Terry cleared his throat, before answering, 'Will you promise to do me a favour and release all the different types of insects, especially the woodlice, if I tell you why the belt is not working for you?'

He followed his speech by performing a belly dance and bellowing loudly like a bull.

Now, words like 'Do me a favour' were often hard for the Emperor to really understand. A sentence starting with the phrase 'Of course your Highness…. straight away' was more to his liking.

The Emperor bit his lip, smiled, and muttered through clenched teeth, 'Of course…. I'm a spider of my word.' He helped the mayor up off the floor.

But the devil inside of Balasz was thinking more evil thoughts, which started and finished with 'Death to all the Dublin insects, especially the woodlice.' He was careful to keep that part of the sentence way down inside his warped mind.

Terry had to think fast on his short hundred, or so, feet, which wasn't easy for a woodlouse that had spent an eternity dangling by the neck.

To be perfectly accurate, woodlice can only think using one half of their brain. The other half is programmed to only see things in black and white pictures. This didn't help with his thought process.

Terry concentrated. He said the second thing that sprang into his mind. The reason it wasn't the first thing was due to the fact that the other half of his brain had projected an image of a fisherman tying up a boat on an island just off Cornwall. So the mayor was about to say, 'You need to tie it in a slipknot,' but he didn't think it was appropriate in the circumstances. Instead he said; 'Has anyone mentioned to you about the special ritual… the ritual called the 'Belt of Kings Ceremony' that needs to take place?'

The Belt of Kings

The Emperor paced back and forth. He glared menacingly across at his 'General for Organising Functions,' who was busy thumbing his way through a copy of the book that described all the 'Rituals of the Insect World'.

There was no mention of this ritual in the Irish section of the big red book.

He shrugged his shoulders towards the Emperor in dismay.

'It's because you haven't been initiated and been given the 'Belt of Kings' by all the heads of the insect families.' Terry said, trying desperately to ensure that his voice didn't appear to be shaking as much as the inside of his body.

'And what does that bloody mean?' The Emperor snapped, while staring dagger eyes at the 'General for Organising Functions.'

Terry could just make out that there was enough doubt in the spider's voice to know that the Emperor was clinging to the last branches on a tree called desperation.

'Advantage woodlouse,' Terry thought.

'But... but there's no mention of that ceremony in the ritual book your Highness,' the general informed everyone in the room.

'Look, your Highness,' Terry walked about, baring his belly button, 'this situation calls for a ceremony, if you want to be the owner of the 'Belt of Kings.' And that ceremony needs to take place when the path of the big, yellow, shiny thing and the big, pale, round thing with a face on it (that both live up in the big blue thing) cross.'

Emperor Balasz backed away from the woodlouse as if he had an incurable disease.

He turned quickly to his 'Brigadier for Communication' and shrugged his shoulders, scratching his head.

'I think its gone mad…. too much hanging about,' said the Emperor. 'Burn it quickly… burn it.'

The Emperor had been told a long time ago that the Irish were not renowned for their intelligence, be that giant or insect. He had also had first hand experience of how dull woodlice were when he met one, back in his homeland. So he imagined that an Irish woodlouse would be way down on the ladder of intellectual thoughts. The Emperor had probably grown flowers that had more brain cells than this ugly low-down bum.

'I think it means…. when the sun and the moon cross in the sky, or, to be more precise, when dusk arrives.' The 'Brigadier from Communication' communicated in a most effective accent.

The Emperor didn't know if he should believe the dull-looking, Irish woodlouse, or get it chopped up and put in to a salad.

Fortunately, for Terry, another shred of skin fell sharply away from the spider's body. This quickly made the Emperor's mind up to go with the suggestion.

'So you are telling me that if I hold a ceremony at dusk with all the heads of the insect families, the 'Belt of Kings' will officially be mine?'

'Yes, it's that simple. All the heads of the insect families just need to kiss the 'Belt,' when the big, yellow, shiny thing...'

'It's the sun... please call it the sun.' Emperor Balasz's patience was at breaking point. Not only was he in a cold strange city, he was slowly dying and, worst of all he was surrounded by idiots, whichever way he looked.

For the first time in his life, Terry's half brain was doing very well. He was thinking clearly and concisely and making it all up as he went along. He knew that Duggan the tailless rat could tell a fairly tall story, but even he'd be proud of this little fable that was racing out of his mouth.

He continued, 'Sorry. OK, your Highness, when the sun...and the.... the...' He looked at the 'Brigadier for Communication,' who thankfully mouthed the word 'Moon' for him.

Terry continued, 'So, when the sun and the moon pass, and the light shines beneath the boardwalk under Pier 14, we lay the belt at your feet with our blessing. Then, according to the ancient insect legend, all the power of the 'Belt of Kings' gets transported to you. You will be its master. It will do what ever you want.'

The sweat dripped off the woodlouse's forehead and splashed onto the floor.

The new 'Apprentice Commander for Finding Things' piped up, 'Emperor are you sure about this story? It sounds a load of old nonsense to me. The sun, moon, rituals... ain't it about time we got a bit realistic here?'

Before he could add another word, Emperor Balasz stormed over to where the new recruit was sitting and blasted out, 'Hey spanner boy... unless you want me to get Mr Bollo to pull off your dungarees and untwist your ballcock... you'd better shut up and sit quiet.'

The rest of the war cabinet smirked at the young upstart.

'It's easier fixing radiators, ain't it?' one of them whispered into the ear of the very young and very naive apprentice spider

If Emperor Balasz had been honest with himself, he would have admitted that he also had a bad feeling about it. But he was desperate, he was falling apart, his hair was dropping out, and his eyes were blurry.

He was starting to regret ever coming on this crusade. He felt like just giving up and buying a nice retirement web down on the coast.

'OK, now listen up... we will carry out the ceremony tomorrow.... but I'm warning you woodlouse... if it doesn't work, I will personally pluck every single leg from your body, and then burn all the tea-chests full of the insects before midnight. We haven't had a good BBQ for a long time.'

The rest of the war cabinet licked their lips in anticipation of the feast.

'Hells bells,' thought Terry, 'why didn't I just keep my big mouth tightly shut?'

Anthony Bunko

Chapter 20

'The Magnificent Three (plus some late comers)'

Emperor Balasz had ordered a huge banquet to take place as soon as the ceremony was finished. His master chef had a restless and sleepless night trying to decide what to prepare to celebrate the Emperor's imminent move into the realms of everlasting eternity.

The chef had finally plumped for a starter of spider and ant broth, with roasted woodlice nibbles, followed by freshly killed bluebottle on a bed of rice, covered in a lemon and lime sauce.

The chef had personally visited the tea-chests to hand select the most succulent pieces of cocooned fly. Unfortunately for Greeneyez, her unusually large coloured eyes had been exactly what the chef had wanted for the centre piece of his proposed magnificent feast. He knew that the Emperor adored his food to be brightly coloured, cooked very rare, with as much blood as possible.

While the cooks were busy slaving away in the kitchens, the heads of all the other insect families were forcefully removed from the tea-chests and brought tearfully to Tiger-Moth Bay, underneath Pier 14.

The prisoners believed that they were going to be killed, sacrificed or, worst of all, sent to somewhere in the Highlands of Scotland.

They were surprised and speechless when they were met by Terry the woodlouse, who was looking rather well, considering that he had been hanging by his neck for over a week. They could see the rope marks around his throat, but didn't understand why he was speaking with a Spanish accent and wriggling his lower half like he needed to use the toilet.

Terry informed them all why they had been personally selected to visit the Emperor's house that afternoon. They didn't know if they should laugh, cry, or just chase him about and strangle the strange, schizophrenic woodlouse for putting them in such grave danger.

'It's quite simple really. It's all part of the ancient 'Kissing the Belt of Kings' ceremony where we pass all the powers over to the Emperor,' he replied cheerfully, before adding a loud 'Ole!'

'A Ceremony…? What ancient 'Kissing the Belt of Kings' Ceremony would that be?' Edmond the ant added his pennyworth to the discussion.

'Look… I made it all up,' Terry answered rather sheepishly in his defence.

'Well that was a stupid thing to make up wasn't it?' Edmond again showed that he was far from impressed. 'What happens when the big, yellow, shiny thing doesn't....?'

Terry stopped him by doing a little belly wriggle. 'It's apparently called the sun,' the woodlouse corrected the ant.

'The what?' Edmond shook his head in disbelief.

'Up there!' Terry pointed to the big, yellow, shiny thing, which was baking hot. 'It's called the sun.'

'Who told you that then?' Edmond folded his arms like a school teacher asking a pupil why he hadn't finished his homework.

'He did.' Terry nodded towards Emperor Balasz who was behind a screen getting changed into a black robe.

'Hmmm.... What else did Mr Know-it-all tell you? Perhaps that the big, pale, shiny thing with a face on it, that replaces the big, yellow, shiny thing, is called Linda Lovelace.'

Terry could see the ant turning to the others and tutting in that annoying way that only ants can do. For two shillings, Terry would have punched his lights out. The ant was really starting to get on the woodlouse's nerves.

'No... actually it's called the moon and, by the way, the other thing that he did tell me,' Terry injected sharply, 'was that tonight he was going to ship the lot of you to his homeland, where he was preparing a massive coming home feast, with you lot as the starter, main course, desert, and finishing off with coffee and insect heads on a stick. Anything else you want to know?' Terry had finally lost his cool.

There was shocked silence amongst the insects, as Terry let his words sink into their thick skulls.

'What happens when that evil Emperor finds out that the ceremony won't make one jot of difference?' The head of the beetle family was first to talk.

They all stared at Terry.

The thinking half of his brain was now starting to hurt with all the reasoning he was doing. 'Uuuugghhh… you all worry too much. I will have thought of something else by then.' Terry's words of comfort only seemed to add more fuel to the total lack of optimism amongst the heads of the insect families.

Suddenly to the sound of trumpets, in marched a battalion of storm-trooper spiders. They were followed by the Emperor; he was being carried on his throne by the massive eunuch spiders. The 'Belt of Kings' gleamed brightly around his waist. The members of his war cabinet shuffled behind.

Emperor Balasz was gently lowered onto the stage. The seven heads of the insect families were summoned over to where he now sat.

Balasz frowned as he watched them scuttle slowly towards him. 'Ugly, dull creatures,' he told himself. 'Why do I need to speak to them? I'll soon have their seven heads mounted on my wall…. for old time's sake.' The devil inside him again spoke the truth. A smile curled up the corner of his mouth.

In the sky, over where the smoke rose from the large brick things, the sun prepared to dip down and go do its job in another part of the world. At the same time, from just behind the metal bridge, which straddled the river, appeared the smiling full face of the moon, (just back from a spot of moonlighting up the other side of the globe). It began its climb up to the top of the darkened Irish sky.

Emperor Balasz sneered wistfully at the insects in front of him. Shivers ran through their skins and shells. Behind them, the big, muscular bodyguard bashed the crab's claw systematically into his great leg, a snarl fixed on his face that would turn coconut milk sour.

The silence was deafening. The atmosphere threatened to explode.

The only sound was the piano music drifting on the night air, from the place where the giant people went to drown their sorrows in barrels of ale.

Terry wished that he was in there now, with his mates, playing poker under the piano.

'Is it time?' Balasz asked Terry, impatiently.

Terry studied the sky; he put his hand on his chin, and lied, 'Not quite yet, your Highness... but not long now.'

The others looked at Terry in admiration.

Just as the Emperor was about to challenge the 'not long now' part of the reply, a commotion at the back of the room, proved to be a pleasant distraction for Terry and his mates.

They glanced through the crowd of black insects. They witnessed two banana spiders dragging behind them what appeared to be the remains of a skinned insect corpse.

Terry noticed straight away that the two banana spiders couldn't have been more different in appearance. They were like chalk and cheese, or ant and beetle.

One was short, quite small boned, with a wheezing chest that made a strange sound like an accordion in the clumsy hands of a novice player. The other was much, much bigger. The size of creature that would even make the giant people step out of the way, or cats scamper for cover.

Emperor Balasz was too pre-occupied with the magical wonder of the belt, to be bothered with such a mundane disturbance that was going on at ground level. He hired bodyguards to sort that kind of stuff out.

Uncle Paddy was of course disguised in one of the suits, which had been expertly made by Mr Zimmermann. But he was finding it terribly hard to move freely. The stitching around his waist had already started to unravel, and his leg-pits were tight and sweating profusely.

It made him move like a gorilla with an extremely bad back.

The noise finally started to get on the Emperor's nerves. This was supposed to be his moment, his greatest triumph, and it was all being spoiled by two odd shaped creatures and a skinned banana spider.

'What is the meaning of this?' Emperor Balasz's voice rose high into the night.

Bongo had instructed Uncle Paddy not to talk, and to only make leg signals if really necessary. Anyway, at least until the third phase of the plan was successfully complete.

Unfortunately, this phase of the well designed plan seemed to be a little flawed. Not only was everyone under pier 14 staring at them, expecting them to speak, but Duggan, who had been despatched to the warehouse where all the teachests were housed, with the intention of releasing all the imprisoned insects to help them overcome the banana spiders, had also just fallen flat on its face.

Stupidly, Duggan, who had all the grace of a sealion, had accidentally tripped over a pebble, alarming the guards. He was caught red-handed, (without putting up too much of a fight), bound in silk thread, and hurriedly marched off in the direction of the ceremony.

Back under the pier, Bollo, the big, muscular spider, leapt off his perch, and shuffled suspiciously over towards the disguised intruders.

'Answer the Emperor!' the spider kicked the dead insect. 'What is this and where did it come from?' He demanded an answer, and quickly.

Bongo stuck to the plan and just looked vacant. His little chest was tighter than it had ever been. He just shook his head. The big spider pushed him hard. Bongo fell backwards.

Suddenly, to add to the drama, Duggan the rat was brought into the arena. Bongo could see that Duggan was all alone and there were no hordes of angry Dublin insects following him and baying for banana spider's blood.

He now wished he had a plan B.

At that moment, Bongo thought that maybe it was time to leg it out of there and perhaps camp out in Sam's Place. It would have been hard enough fighting Balasz and his army with all the insects that Dublin could have mustered, but now, with only three of them, it was leaning on the side of impossible.

Emperor Balasz looked bored and with all this waiting he was ready to explode at any moment. 'What now?' he shrieked.

'We found this one sniffing around the warehouse,' one of the soldiers informed him.

Bollo, the big, muscular spider, could tell something was going on. He could smell suspicion in the air. He spun around sharply to face Uncle Paddy. He was impressed with the size of the spider standing tall in front of him. He wondered where he worked out and how much he could bench press.

'You! What happened?' he poked the ex-street fighter. 'Where did you find this body?'

Uncle Paddy shrugged his shoulders, puffed out his chest and made a strange grinding sound with his teeth.

Bongo had an uncomfortable and nasty feeling about what would happen next. He had heard his uncle grind his teeth a thousand times, which normally meant that a right royal punch-up was about to happen.

The big, muscular spider was not used to other spiders puffing their chest out so threateningly and sticking up for themselves. The slap from Bollo's strong leg was aimed at Uncle Paddy's head, to show the crowd who was the boss. The punch missed its intended target by a mile, as the old street fighter ducked, and then sent a rabbit punch into the bodyguard's rib-cage, followed by another one to the jaw. Bollo was instantly floored.

This caused a wave of shocked disbelief to ride over the place.

By this time Bongo knew that his plan was well and truly doomed, especially when Uncle Paddy started to rip his costume off his broad shoulders and roll up the sleeves of his remaining seven legs.

He was itching for a brawl.

'So it's another rumble you'll be a-wanting?' the spider's thick Irish accent pierced the night sky, 'and this time without the sand.'

'I told you not to worry,' Terry the woodlouse turned and spat the words at his so-called colleagues. 'We're safe now. Paddy 'O' Dacey, the greatest street-fighting spider that Ireland has ever produced, is here to the rescue.'

As soon as he said that, Uncle Paddy tripped over his discarded costume and was instantly jumped on by ten banana spiders, who proceeded to pin him to the floor.

There was uproar, as all hell was let loose. Bongo ran to help his poor uncle.

'Duggan!' Bongo shouted, 'give us a hand!'

The rat easily broke out of the webbing that was holding him. But he took one look at the big, muscular bodyguard spider, who had staggered back onto his legs and stopped dead in his tracks.

The cowardly rodent turned and fled towards the big, blue wet thing. He skipped passed several soldier spiders holding pine-cones as he sprinted through the crowd, weaving and dodging as he escaped through a section of broken sewage pipe and shouted out, 'I'll be back!', just before getting washed out into the big, blue wet thing that was slightly murky from the sewage of the giant people.

'Duggan… you chicken!' Bongo yelled after him, as three seriously mean looking banana spiders chased the teenage spider around a wooden pier post.

'Get them.' Emperor Balasz pointed towards the two spiders in disguise, 'I don't care if they are dead or alive.'

Before anyone could move, Bollo, the big, muscular bodyguard, got gingerly back to his feet, shook his head, spat his two front teeth out and grunted, 'He's mine… leave the big one to me.'

The other banana spiders backed away from the daddy long-legs.

Uncle Paddy smiled directly back at the spider.

The Belt of Kings

Balasz didn't really have time for all this big spider macho stuff. He again turned to ask Terry the woodlouse if it was time for the ritual to begin.

Obviously Terry's answer was negative. The insect mayor loved to watch a good scrap, and they didn't come much bigger than Paddy 'O' Dacey verses the Muscles from Bogotá.

'OK then,' Emperor Balasz gave his permission for Bollo to fight. 'But make it quick and as bloody as possible.' He sat back on his throne to observe the spectacle.

A large circle was made as the two street hardened warriors limbered up.

An older banana spider sauntered up to Uncle Paddy and asked him to choose weapons. The daddy long-legs looked in the basket and there was an assortment of vicious looking objects. There were darning needles, pine-cones, rose thorns and little pebbles wrapped in web-spit.

Uncle Paddy stared across to the large bodyguard, who had selected an extra-sharp sword made out of river reed. 'Hey Bollo... What about just using these?' He held up his clenched pads.

'Fine by me... you are the one who is going to die whatever we use.' The large muscular bodyguard grinned and snapped the reed sword in half.

Uncle Paddy untangled himself from the last piece of the costume. Bongo was being held back by two soldier spiders.

The two street-wise fighters circled each other, never breaking eye contact. Bongo could feel the hatred, mixed with pure respect between the two boxing warriors.

'Booshhhh.' A solid blow from Bollo connected firmly with Uncle Paddy's chin.

The daddy long-legs was dazed. It was followed automatically by another, and then another to the body.

'Bollo….. Bollo… Bollo,' loud chants rang out from the crowd.

'Knock his big, ugly block off,' Terry the woodlouse screamed, but he went quiet when he saw the Emperor giving him one of his evil red eyed stares.

Uncle Paddy was sadly missing his old slugging leg, which regretfully hung redundant on the wall behind the Emperor.

He couldn't find his rhythm. Blood trickled from his nose into his mouth.

The yells from the crowd grew louder and louder.

Another sharp jab connected with Uncle Paddy. He staggered backwards, knocking over five or six onlookers.

Bongo was concerned; he found it hard to watch his Uncle getting roasted. Uncle Paddy was backed up, leaning on a metal can, as the bodyguard punched the ex-street fighter's body relentlessly.

'Paddy,' Terry shouted above the noise, 'get off the can… he's killing you…. get off the can… bob and weave… bob and weave.' The woodlouse made shadow-boxing motions up on the stage, in between the belly dancing routine.

'It's a massacre,' Edmond the ant interjected. 'He's getting slaughtered. Terry, I thought you said that he was the greatest. He's just a useless bum.'

'Perhaps he's not feeling himself,' Terry replied sorrowfully, now realising they were now all doomed to tragically end up, as the main ingredients in a banana spider's homemade pie.

But what nobody noticed in the packed arena was the wide smile that was planted on Uncle Paddy's face. Also, what no one could hear above the noise and the excitement was the words that the daddy long-legs was whispering into the ear of the tiring muscular spider.

'It's not hurting,' He mocked the bodyguard. 'Is that all you've got Bollo?' he taunted. 'You're an ugly old brute, you've got a face like the raw behind of a centipede, and you hit like a girly worm.'

Now there are several things that one spider can say to another without giving too much offence. But actually calling someone such insulting comments in public during a punch-up was without doubt the most insulting thing ever to say to a creature with eight legs.

Uncle Paddy didn't care two hoots. He was really enjoying it. He just laughed and dished out some more verbal insults as he soaked up more physical punishment.

This made the bodyguard try twice as hard, but subsequently tire three times as fast.

As cagey as a tiger hiding in the long grass, Uncle Paddy was waiting for the right moment to pounce.

'Come on ugly.' He mocked.

'BANG', Bollo's fists connected with Uncle Paddy's ribs.

'Is that all you've got. I've been hit harder by a money spider.' It was getting personal.

'BASH', the bodyguard swung wildly.

Then at the right moment, and as the bodyguard slowly moved in swinging a tired looking punch, Uncle Paddy side-stepped out of the way, turned his attacker around onto the old rusty can and connected with several savage punches that firstly staggered, and then floored the big beast from the rain forest.

'WOW,' was the common cry.

Uncle Paddy raised up his two sets of front legs (obviously minus the leg which had been pulled off) in triumph above his head. He danced around the ring performing his famous old 'Uncle Paddy shuffle.'

'Yessss…,' shouted Bongo, breaking free from his captives and racing over to congratulate his uncle. 'He's out cold…. you won…. you won, Uncle Paddy… you are the greatest.'

'Easy. I told you I would beat him, even with one leg tied onto the wall over there.' He pointed at his old slugging leg, which was attached to the palace wall.

In the background, Terry the woodlouse had climbed onto the large wooden pillar. He proceeded to flash his belly button at everyone and poke his tongue out at Edmond the ant.

Anthony Bunko

Chapter 21

'Now it's the Magnificent six (or is it seven?)'

Although the Emperor was taken aback by the way that Bollo had been unceremoniously despatched by the large daddy long-legs, he just couldn't wait any longer. All this fooling around and playing macho spiders was making him more irritable.

He snatched the 'Belt of Kings' off the table and demanded that the heads of the insect families kiss it and present it to him immediately.

'But it's not quite time,' muttered Terry hopefully.

'Look, just do it… and stop wriggling your belly button, or I'll stick this darning needle straight through it.' The Emperor's patience had finally snapped.

The heads of the insect families all did what they were asked to do, even though they knew it wouldn't make a blind bit of difference.

When the Emperor had the freshly blessed 'Belt' in his grasp he commanded his henchmen to kill the lot of them, starting with Uncle Paddy, and finishing with the slow and painful death of the irritating woodlouse.

'And make sure it's as bloody possible.' Balasz wrapped the belt around his body and sat down on his throne, waiting for the powers to work.

'Arrrrrggh, Arrrrrggh,' Duggan yelled, as he swung from a rope under the pier, like Tarzan to the rescue.

Unfortunately, the airborne rodent sailed straight past where all the action was taking place, and collided with a wooden post. Dust shook from the rafters

Duggan groggily jumped to his feet, 'I told you I'd be back,' he informed an amazed Bongo,

'Where did you go?' Bongo shouted, as the army of banana spiders circled around them, ready to attack.

'I went for help… and look who I found?' The rat lowered his snout and down slid Eric, the cross-dressing slow-worm, kitted out in a bright orange earwig uniform, with matching boots and balaclava.

He was followed by the mad, tongue-less Welsh caterpillar with the large head.

'Heard you were in a spot of trouble, kid,' Eric muttered, as they stared at the advancing mass of black insects. Eric added, 'and by the way, there's definitely too much black around here; let's start to brighten this place up a bit.'

'Mmmmmmrgh,' grunted the mad, tongue-less Welsh caterpillar with the big head, whilst breaking into a particularly strange war dance, and baring his big white teeth.

'Glad to have you on board,' Bongo said, as the killer spiders closed in.

But inwardly he knew that an extra two warriors was not going to make much difference in the outcome of the battle. They could really have done with some more help. Perhaps with an entire army of mad, tongue-less, Welsh caterpillars with large heads; that would have evened the score a little.

'Oh...,' interrupted Duggan, 'I nearly forgot who I went to find in the first place.' His whistle sailed out loudly above the great wall of noise.

Then, out from the shadows, a figure emerged that seemed to block out the big, yellow, shiny thing.

Bongo rubbed his eyes, not believing what he was seeing. He was speechless.

'I can't believe it,' the teenage spider finally managed to find some words to string together.

The reason for his disbelief was there standing tall, in all his glory, was no other than the chief of the rat colony that lived underneath a village in Zambolo and who actually had a real zebra bone in his nose.

Bongo shrugged his shoulders at Duggan, who, of course, was standing there wearing the biggest and smuggest grin across his face.

The rat spoke, 'I told you he was real... didn't I?'

'Welcome aboard.' Uncle Paddy shook the chief's paws. 'I like the real zebra bone. Let's go and kick some banana spider butt,' Uncle Paddy shouted.

Within the blink of an eye, the two groups clashed.

Claws flashed, legs kicked and blood flowed. Wave upon wave of hairy black banana spider attacks were dispelled by the magnificent few.

Uncle Paddy and the African chief rat were immense. They despatched their attackers with ease. Uncle Paddy smiled and hollered with glee, like a child bouncing on a trampoline, as he piled into a fresh battalion of on-coming spiders.

'I haven't had a good scrap like this since those flying ants came over on a ferry for the weekend from the Isle of Man.' He lashed out with a vicious uppercut that nearly decapitated a poor banana spider.

Bongo was also earning his fighting stripes.

He had been hit a few times, but all-in-all, he was holding his own. So was Eric, who was on the shoulders of the mad, tongue-less Welsh caterpillar with the large head, swatting the enemy with a large plank of timber.

Even Terry the woodlouse, along with several of the other heads of the insect family, had decided to join in and fight their corner.

But however gallantly the unlikely heroes fought, Bongo knew that they would soon tire under the relentless attacks of the banana spiders.

He watched in horror, as Terry the woodlouse was engulfed under a mass of black bodies. Also Eric, the gallant slow-worm, was pulled from his companions shoulders and they were both being driven back towards the edge of the pier.

Up on the stage, still barking orders, was Emperor Balasz, anxiously waiting for the belt to begin its magic.

Unbelievably, Duggan had done more hiding than fighting. He eventually popped up from behind an old rusty can of peaches and raced wildly through the crowd, again heading in the wrong direction.

'Where are you going now?' Bongo cried after the rat, as two of Emperor's troops edged towards the young spider brandishing deadly looking pine-cones.

'I'll be back,' the deserting rodent replied.

'Not again,' Uncle Paddy commented. 'That will be his catchphrase if he's not careful.'

They watched the tailless rat disappear into the darkening night for the second time.

Thankfully, there followed a well deserved lull in the fighting for everyone to take stock and get their breath back.

The magnificent heroes had been forced back and now formed themselves into a small circle. The black spider soldiers surrounded them.

Bongo was very afraid. There were hairy black creatures with death in their eyes everywhere he looked.

This time the troops didn't rush forward aimlessly. This time they had been ordered to inch forwards as one powerful and unstoppable unit, towards the sorry looking band of Irish insects,

'Watch yourself, Bongo,' his Uncle Paddy said, purposely moving in between his young, teenage nephew and the on-coming army. 'Look boy.... make a run for it... I'll try to fend them off. Go save yourself... you're too young to die!'

'No way Uncle Paddy... I've got us into this mess... I'm staying.' Bongo moved back to take his place in the frontline.

'Good kid,' Uncle Paddy said, knowing that Bongo's old man would have been proud. The ex-street fighter added, 'Ok... but watch your back and only punch when you see the reds of their eyes.'

The banana spiders banged their chests aggressively. The small band of brave Dublin insects could now taste the fear in the air and smell the stench of death that hang around under Pier 14.

Without warning, Terry the woodlouse started to sing at the top of his voice:

> *'Insects of Dublin,*
> *We stand together,*
> *In the face of this stormy weather,*
> *Although we are few,*
> *We will never,*
> *Give in to our enemy.*
>
> *Creatures of Dublin,*

The Belt of Kings

We must stand and fight,
Against Balasz and all his might,
They may be many,
But we know what's right,
And we will overcome

We will fight for Dublin,
Uncle Paddy will bash their heads in,
It's our destiny to be free,
And all our children to see the beauty
of the city that we live in,
Now Insects of Dublin,
Let's stand together,
Father, mother, sister, brother,
On this day we will endeavour,
To set Dublin free

The rest joined in the third verse and chorus, except the mad, tongue-less Welsh caterpillar with the large head, who instead clambered onto a large box and started doing his now familiar (and very odd) style of traditional Irish jugging.

The banana spiders' stopped to watch and listen in amazement at the strange sight and sounds of the small band of creatures. After another two verses of the song the banana spiders decided that enough was enough and continued their advance.

Bongo could feel the breath of the spider army drift towards him. It somehow stuck to his skin. He knew he had to be brave.

Emperor Balasz stood up and held up his leg, ready to give the order for his troops to conquer and destroy the pests.

Suddenly, from way off in the distance, a thunderous noise could be heard by all. It grew and grew. It seemed to be heading in their direction.

'What's that?' Terry the woodlouse asked, whacking a banana spider over the head with a pot.

'It sounds like one of them tram-machines that the giant people travel on.' Eric commented.

'Mmmmmrghhhh,' agreed the mad, tongue-less Welsh caterpillar with the large head.

Bongo listened. He hoped the sound was what he thought it was. It reminded him of the same sound that he had heard on the day that he and Greeneyez had played on the corpse of the dead giant.

The wall of sound was descending their way. Everyone's head turned to see what or who was causing the commotion.

Then they appeared; thousands upon thousands of insects of every size, shape and colour; wave upon wave of creatures like a blanket covering the floor. And leading at the front of the stampeding throng, with a smile as wide as the River Liffy, was Duggan the rat.

'I told you I'd be back,' he shouted to his mates.

Emperor Balasz was really starting to dislike these Irish insects. Why couldn't they just roll over and accept defeat like the cowardly creatures in his country?

The insects that Duggan had freed from the tea-chests were in a very bad mood. They had been locked up in cramped conditions for a long time, and now someone was going to pay. They were all tooled-up in anticipation of a right royal dust-up. Pieces of wood, bits of thorns, and numerous apple stalks were carried with the intention of breaking banana spider's heads.

The newly-freed insects stopped in one line as they saw the banana spiders surrounding Bongo and the rest of the brave mixture of Dublin's creatures.

A crazed earwig, with a mop of ginger hair and eyes that were on fire, held up his two hundred and fifty-one toes on all his left feet. He shouted loud and proud, 'Are you ready insects of Dublin?'

'YES!' came back the much louder reply from the band of insects.

'Well OK….it's 'getting our own back' time,' he yelled, 'CHARGE!'

There was an explosion of sound as insects clashed with insects with the odd rat or two thrown in between for good measure.

The fighting was intense.

Being locked up and nearly starved to death in the tea-chests had given the Irish insects the extra inner-strength that was just the edge they needed to quickly overcome their more illustrious counterparts.

Ten minutes later most of the banana spiders lay dead, dying, or had their legs up in surrender. It was over. Dublin was back in the legs, hands, antennae and wings of its rightful owners. Loud cheers sailed up through the wooden floorboards of pier 14 as the Irish insects hugged and kissed each other in triumph.

A small giant boy, who had witnessed the entire battle while peeping through the floorboards above the pier, rushed to tell his parents of the struggle.

'What did you see?' his father asked, staring worryingly at the boy's mother.

'I saw a massive daddy long-legs beat up an equally big banana spider. There was a big black rat with, I think, but I'm not really sure, a real zebra bone in his nose, and there was a slow-worm who was dressed as an earwig. It was great dad. What a battle!' The boy's face was beaming.

'That's it; he's never going to visit your mad Aunty Zelda in the country again; and stop feeding him all those potatoes.' The father stormed off from the rest of the family and sat alone licking an ice-cream at the far edge of pier 14.

When the celebrations had subsided under pier 14, Terry the woodlouse asked about the whereabouts of the 'Belt of Kings,' and the evil Emperor Balasz.

All eyes glanced towards the stage where they could plainly see a figure hiding behind the throne.

'Come out Bal-hash!' Terry demanded.

'It's Balasz…. It's Emperor Balasz,' the evil tyrant said defiantly.

'Well, sorry Balasz…. there's no Emperor around here no more,' Terry's words were met with loud applause. 'Now come out here like a real spider and take your punishment.'

There were genuine gasps of horror, as the shadowy figure of the once all-powerful Emperor appeared from behind the chair. He was still clutching the 'Belt of Kings' in his ageing legs.

The ritual that had been made-up by the woodlouse, obviously hadn't worked because Balasz looked like a very old spider, all wrinkled and grey. Chunks of moulted skin hung off him like leaves on a tree on a blustery autumn day.

He could hardly hold the belt in his spindly legs. He announced through clenched teeth to the shocked crowd of insects that he was sorry.

'It's too late to be sorry now,' Bongo said, taking the belt out of his grasp. 'What shall we do with him?' he yelled towards the crowd.

'Kill him!' shouted the new 'Apprentice Commander for Finding Things,' who was standing at the side with the rest of the prisoners, front legs on his head.

'Pluck off his legs,' the 'Second-lieutenant for Making Him Feel Good' screamed with all his might.

'Pop his head…. Pop his head,' said the 'Minister for Dishing Out Punishment.'

Bongo thought that if these were the Emperor's so called friends, he wouldn't like to meet his enemies.

There was lots of shouting and yelling as everyone seemed to have an opinion on what should be done with the evil spider.

The talking and muttering stopped as a strange pong rose up to greet them all.

'What's that smell?' Uncle Paddy motioned to Bongo, holding his nose.

'I don't know… It smells like rotten fish and terrible body odour.'

Then from the back of the room, from where the smell had originated, there was a sound of water and clip-clopping of tiny claws.

The crowd of insects at the back, moved out of the way.

Bongo shrugged his shoulders in confusion towards his uncle. But Emperor Balasz had recognised the smell immediately. He started to shake. It was his worse nightmare coming back to haunt him.

Across the sands trotted the clawless crab that Balasz had had savagely beaten earlier and dumped in the cold waters. The crab's eyes never left the Emperors, as he shuffled sideways onto the stage. He picked up his own amputated claw, which hung on the wall next to Uncle Paddy's slugger. He slotted it back into his claw socket, snapping it open and shut several times, to ensure that it was working.

'I wish I could do that,' Uncle Paddy reached for his arm on the wall.

Emperor Balasz tried unsuccessfully to scuttle away.

The crab turned to Terry and Bongo and asked in a very polite tone, 'Do you mind, if I take him with me?'

They both nodded their heads in acceptance at the crab's request.

'But what are you going to do with him?' Bongo asked.

'I just want to take him for a dip in the sea... where he doesn't belong!' the crab replied quite sarcastically.

They were all enthralled as they watched the sea creature pick the Emperor off the ground by the throat. There was a loud 'Oohhh' from everyone present as the crab majestically and viciously rubbed the Emperor's head into his smelly armpit, before shuffling to the edge of the pier and hopping off into the big, blue wet thing.

The silence hung around for several moments.

It was finally broken when a voice from somewhere in the arena shouted out. 'Bongo.... Bongo.'

He recognised it instantly. It was Greeneyez. The young spider's eyes searched the large crowd of insects.

Then he saw her cocooned on a large plate on the banquet table. Greeneyez was trying unsuccessfully to wave to him. He raced over, his heart beating fast. When he reached the pretty fly, he pulled the webbing off her, picked her up and held her tight in his legs.

'You took your time…incey…wincey.' She smirked.

They both laughed and held each other tight. Just then the mad, tongue-less Welsh caterpillar with the large head, leaped up on a barrel and somehow started an almighty sing-song that lasted well into the long sunnytime night.

Chapter 22

'Sunnytime blues'

The big, shiny, yellow thing, (which had now been officially renamed the big, shiny, sunny, yellow thing), had risen up in the big blue thing, (which still had its original title), at least seven times since the evil Emperor Balasz had been despatched to the bottom of the big wild wet blue thing with the smelly crab with body odour.

The rest of the banana spiders had been packed tightly up into the tea-chests and shipped back to the darkest rain forests of South America, with instructions written in large letters, 'Do Not Open 'til Springtime.'

Now life down on the dockside was slowly, but surely, getting back to normal. The 'Belt of Kings' had been polished and returned to its rightful place in the vaults.

Duggan, Bongo and Uncle Paddy were given the freedom of the Tiger-Moth Bay for their part in saving all of the dockside insects from becoming takeaway lunches in some backstreet shop in the rainforest of darkest South America. They were treated like heroes wherever they went.

Even Eric and Big Taff were cheered and clapped whenever they ventured out of Sam's Place. Eric had even made it acceptable for cross-dressing insects to come out of the cemetery. Every new day more and more cross dressers insects were seen out on the streets.

As the days moved on, Bongo had spent most of his time with Greeneyez. They had done lots of teenage things together. Spider ballooning, crawling up a pipe and spider abseiling, but today, Bongo was going to achieve his lifetime ambition of flying high above the city.

Although keen, he was also extremely nervous, as he left his boot home and headed to meet his girl-fly for the afternoon.

Along the way, he couldn't help but notice Duggan, who was sitting on a small box, explaining to a gang of insect kids, how the battle of the 'Belt of Kings' had been won.

Bongo hid in a doorway to listen to what story would escape from the mouth of the likeable vermin.

'Mr Duggan, please tell us again,' a small bright-eyed beetle kid, who couldn't have been much out of larvae, asked.

'Oh, come on now kids, you know I don't like to brag, but if you really want to hear the tale of the greatest rescue this city has ever seen, who am I to disappoint you all.' The rat tilted his head forward, so they wouldn't miss a single word. 'Well you see, it was like this. Time was running out. The rest of the boys were taking a terrible beating, so it was up to me to save the day.'

Bongo watched in amusement.

Duggan continued, 'I marched right up to that evil Emperor, looked him squarely in his nasty red eyes, and said.....' before he had chance to complete his speech, all the kids had yelled back.

'I'll be back!'

Duggan laughed, and pointed to his hat, which had his now famous saying written on it in big letters.

'Yes... I said I'll be back. And back I came, and we kicked that Emperor and his sorry looking-spiders all the way out of Dublin City.'

The googly-eyed kid insects cheered and hugged the tailless rodent. Bongo waved at his mate as he went on his way. The young spider headed onwards towards Greeneyez' home.

He entered Buzztown, but the welcome he received was much different to the first time he had ventured through the archway.

Flies clapped him, called his name, or offered him revolting pieces of regurgitated food (which he politely declined). He picked up his girl-fly and they raced off towards the end of the pier and stopped at the edge.

'Are you ready?' she asked, noticing the fearful expression rooted firmly on his face.

'As ready as I'll ever be.' He swallowed hard as he stared at the big, wild, wet blue thing that glistened uninvitingly below.

'Well jump on board,' she said.

Bongo climbed onto her back. She could feel him shaking.

'Hope I don't drop you like I dropped my brother. He got swallowed up by a large fishy thing with enormous teeth,' she joked.

He poked her hard. She ran towards the edge.

His legs held around her tightly, his eyes closed even tighter. Then they were off. Bongo, still with his eyes shut, couldn't hear a sound. He finally opened three eyes, and found himself floating high above the cold water below.

It was unusually peaceful and quiet.

He immediately noticed the lack of sound. Everything seemed to be moving down below in slow motion.

'You can stop choking me now,' she struggled to get her words out. 'Well? What do you think then, incey wincey?'

He was again lost for words. As they glided between buildings which appeared to reach up at least a thousand miles into the big blue thing, he'd never seen anything so beautiful,

He was amazed how vast the city was. It stretched as far as his eyes could see. On the Eastside, black smoke bellowed from large chimneys, and rusty cranes sat overlooking the shipyard. Towards the Westside, he could see the bright green grass, where the worms slithered about.

This was the most exciting thing he had ever done, and that included saving Dublin from an evil tyrant spider. It was miles better than crawling down the sewage system tunnels, or lassoing another insect, or catching his first victim in his homemade web.

They flew about for ages. She took him to all the places that he had never seen before.

'It is a different world up here,' he thought. 'I wished I had wings. I wonder if Mr Zimmermann could make me some? No…. no that's too weird,' he decided.

For lunch she landed smack in the middle of a sticky cream cake that took centre stage in a cake shop window. They rested and feasted until a giant with a rolled up piece of paper and a tighter rolled-up scowl angrily chased them away.

The best part for Bongo was when the sun started to fade and was replaced by a million gas-lights across the city. Bongo had never seen anything like it. Trams and automobiles snaked below them.

Bongo was too excited to have noticed the cold wind that was creeping up from the coastline and hiding in the corner's of the alleyways.

They finally landed just outside Bongo's boot home at quarter past nine. His mother made the two love-bugs some lumps of cheese and lemonade for supper.

It was a grand end to a perfect day.

'That was fantastic,' Bongo commented.

'Thanks… what shall we do tomorrow?' Greeneyez arched her aching back.

'Lets go flying again… perhaps you could take me to see….' He was stopped in his tracks by her exhausted expression.

'Oh… incey, wincey… I'm not your Uncle Paddy. I'm not made of muscle… I'll need a rest.'

'Oh, sorry,' he wasn't thinking straight. 'I know lets go to the cinema, then I'll take you to swim in a giant's toilet. You wouldn't believe the rush you have when they flush the cistern. Hope you won't get toilet sickness.'

'What about going to Insect Forgotten City?' she asked. 'I'd love to go to Sam's Place, and see Big Taff and Eric again.'

'I don't know. It's no place for a lady. We'll see.' He left it at that for the moment.

They kissed in the moonlight.

He knew that the rest of his family would be sneaking a peek at them from out of the lace holes of the boot. But he didn't care.

He watched as she gracefully flew away into the night sky.

'See you tomorrow,' he shouted after her.

In turn she circled in the sky and wrote the words 'OK incey wincey' in cloud dust.

All his brothers and sisters burst out laughing, while their older brother's cheeks filled up with embarrassment.

Chapter 23

'Here comes the……..'

Bongo didn't know if it was because of all the fresh air from flying all day, or the cheese slices he had for supper, but he had wonderful dreams during the night. Thankfully, it was the first time since the whole episode had ended that there was not a hairy black banana spider scurrying around in his mind.

At first, he had dreamt that he was a giant person, strolling about the city, taller than the tallest building. Later on, he imagined that he was swimming in the big, wet, blue thing, but was pleased when he fell out of bed and woke up just at the moment that he was about to be swallowed up by a big fishy thing with large teeth.

He got off the floor and climbed back into his cosy bed. His little heart was too full of warmth to have noticed the cold wind that had sneaked into the city overnight. He was too wrapped up in his memories to have noticed the difference in the air.

He turned over in his hammock and snuggled under the blankets, trying desperately to return to dreamland.

'Get up lazy bones,' he heard his mother calling him from outside his room.

He didn't answer. He closed his eyes instead.

He heard her enter his room, and rummage about. She continued doing the normal things that all mothers in the world, be it giants or insects, did. She moaned and groaned, and huffed and puffed her way into every untidy corner of the bedroom.

Bongo was still half asleep as he turned to discuss something with her.

'Aaaargh,' he let out a cry. 'Mam… what is that….? Why have you got it out?' He pointed at the freshly washed and ironed beetle's costume that his mother was holding up.

'Look Bongo, Sunnytime is over.' She threw the suit onto the bed. 'The cold white flakes of snow fell from the big blue thing last night, when we were all sleeping.'

She yanked back the tongue of the boot, to reveal a city covered in a blanket of thick white snow.

'But… but I'm supposed to be taking Greeneyez to the cinema, then swimming in a toilet bowl.'

His mother hung the costume on the cupboard and said, 'There will be no Greeneyez, and no more lounging about in the cinema watching films. Well, not until next year anyway. So come on, you're the father of the family now, hero or no hero; there are seventy-eight mouths to be fed down there, so get up and get in disguise.

He felt like screaming.

He scampered up to the entrance of the boot-top. His eyes scanned the streets. He was hoping to see the centipede strolling with the earwig, or black ants and red ants hanging out on the corner, but the pavements were empty.

Up by the Chinese linen basket he observed a working spider getting the big sign ready (which would flash to warn everyone that they were under beetle attack).

'It was really over,' he thought sadly. Cree-season had slipped through his little pads without him realising it.

He glanced up at the big blue thing just in time to see Cyril the seagull swooping down in search of his first piece of insect meat of the wintertime. Luckily for Bongo he missed. The terrified spider dived for cover

The young teenager hid under his blankets, heart beating and his chest getting tighter and tighter. He prayed for it to be sunnytime again, even for a day, so he could say goodbye to Greeneyez properly.

His mother popped back in and firmly said, 'Bongo get up this minute. Hurry up, and you can take your younger brother, Eugene, with you this year. We have a spare beetle's costume in the cupboard, and make sure you bring him back in one piece. Don't let him start drinking in those places where the giant people go.'

With that thought planted in his mind, Bongo slowly got out of bed, wiped a stray tear from his many sets of eyes and started to squeeze into the beetle's costume.

'Hey, perhaps I will get Mr Zimmermann to make me a bluebottle costume so I can sneak over to Buzztown and see Greeneyez on the weekends,' he said to himself and let go of a devilish smile.

He then shouted to his brother to get ready to go scavenging down the unfriendly streets of Tiger-Moth Bay.

THE END

*Thanks for taking the time to read the
'Belt of Kings'
Hope you enjoyed!*

"And don't forget… next time you glance down and see a spider scuffling menacingly across the carpet, just stop and ask yourself…
- ❖ Is it off to scavenge morsels of food from the beetles?
- ❖ Or is it going on a wonderful date with a gorgeous fly?
- ❖ Or for the truly weird ones out there….is it really a transsexual earth-worm just coming back from visiting Mr Zimmermann?"

The underworld is a strange and wonderful place

I would like to send out a massive 'Thank You' to

Vince Kerr, Phil Shelley and Lyn Williams.

Forever in your debt.